Punk Rock Cowgirl

Punk Rock Cowgirl

A Blackberry Cove Romance

Kasey Lane

TULE
PUBLISHING

To Kaylie, Megan, and Maisey for helping me through a really rough year with a few tears and a lot of laughter.

Chapter One

KENDALL KELLY WAS the queen of her stage. No one could accuse her of not knowing how to play a role. Whether the part was that of audacious punk princess, the fallen-from-grace overindulgent rock star, or the small-town girl from the other side of the tracks, Kendall went all in and owned it because the second she showed a twinge of doubt was the moment they'd all swoop in and take her out at the knees.

Walking into her grandmother's memorial service had started out the same way, with her playing the role that was expected of her. This time she was the shamed, but grieving granddaughter to the last remaining member of her family. Her grandmother, well-known curmudgeon and all-around town witch, was Kendall's last tenuous link to this dusty backwater town. Unless she counted her soon-to-be ex-husband, which she didn't, everyone else had either moved on and forgotten their Blackberry Cove roots...or they'd simply died. So much dust in the wind. That was her family.

And up until last week when she'd received the somber email from her grandmother's lawyer, she'd been a small speck of that dust out there trying to salvage what was left of her sad shooting star of a career—a career that she'd never really pursued or wanted. But now she found herself walking into the dark town church that had seen just about every wedding—shotgun or otherwise—baptism, and funeral of this forgotten hellhole for the last one hundred years. Well, every wedding except hers. Her nuptials had taken place in a nauseatingly pink chapel in Las Vegas on her eighteenth birthday.

But this was definitely not the time to think about her marriage. Or the lack thereof of her relationship with her quote-unquote husband. Kendall ran her hand over her head, checking to make sure every pale pink hair was in place; which of course it was since the gallon of hairspray she'd lacquered on every strand pretty much guaranteed it wouldn't budge even if a hurricane hit the church. No, this morning she would focus on getting through a memorial for a woman who never once told Kendall she loved her, never once read her a bedtime story, and had only reminded her on a daily basis what a drain of money and energy Kendall was on her.

And yet, Kendall thought ruefully, *you ran back to her every time she asked you to despite her constant berating and belittling.*

Kendall hated funerals, and this was her second in under a year. Her half-sister, Sabre, had died tragically in a freak motorcycle accident up in Portland. Kendall had flown out for the service, still in shock and mourning the idea of their lost relationship more than anything since Sabre's father had raised her older sister—a relation the two sisters didn't share. The sharp ache in her chest throbbed thinking of her beautiful, talented sibling gone. Just like everyone else.

In the airport restroom Kendall had donned a tight, but modest black wrap dress because she was playing a role after all, but she drew the line at her boots when it came to her newfound modesty. She refused to give up her rhinestone cowboy boots even for a funeral. Her boots may be her signature to the rest of the world, but to Kendall they were armor, armor she'd need to protect her from whispered insults and not-so-hidden looks of disgust because although there wasn't one person in attendance who claimed Mary Ellen Kelly as a friend or even a decent neighbor since her grandmother had never had a kind word for anyone in town, damned if the good folks of Humboldt County, California, didn't love themselves a spectacle. And the reappearance of their bad girl gone worse would definitely prove to be a drama. Even better would be the reunion of said bad girl with the town's golden boy she'd left behind barely two years after she married him and then ripped out his heart.

Ignoring the acid bubbling in her gut she threw back her shoulders and stomped into the full church. She didn't bother glancing at the filled pews, nevertheless she could feel their eyes on her, trying to cut her down to size and tear her off the high horse they all claimed she rode around on. A murmured spiteful word here and there hit her like stabby little pinpricks: too good, trash, whore, arrogant, cheater. It hurt now just like it always had. But she couldn't control what people said about her; she'd never been able to even with the town's favorite son by her side, so she certainly wasn't going to now.

No matter. She wasn't here for anyone but herself. She wouldn't have even bothered to show in the first place if Nana's lawyer hadn't insisted she meet him after the service for the reading of her grandmother's will. And it's not like her one remaining friend in this godforsaken town would make an appearance at her grandmother's funeral since she'd been meaner to Delilah than just about anyone else. And that was quite an achievement as Nana was equally horrid to everyone in town.

She snorted to herself as she found a seat in the empty front bench. Will. Like her grandmother had anything other than that dying sinkhole of dirt to will to anyone. And Kendall was the last of their family, unless anyone had been able to locate her Uncle Jim who'd taken off before she'd been born. Kendall planned to have the dilapidated farmhouse and surrounding forty acres on the market before sundown tomorrow, right before she left Blackberry Cove in her dust for the last time.

She folded her clammy hands neatly in her lap, wanting desperately to rub them on her dress. But she wouldn't. She couldn't. They didn't need to know how uncomfortable she was in her own hometown, that she was far more afraid of them than they had ever been of her. Breathing deeply, she counted to ten and pretended the heavy, unseasonably hot spring air that filled her lungs was fresh and cool. She would get through this, get rid of that damn house, and get the hell of town before she had a chance to stir up the ghostly husks of her past.

Seconds before the service was scheduled to begin, the rumble of whispered voices halted, words left hanging in the air like more of that damn dust that seemed to cling to everything in Blackberry Cove. She wanted to turn, but she couldn't. Wouldn't. She knew exactly who was creating the clamor at the back of the church. And she wasn't giving him any more power over her than he'd already gathered. Yes, she was the town Jezebel, but no one really knew their story except for them. And maybe she was a lot less golden and a helluva lot more tarnished than he was, but they didn't know the truth. Hell, even he didn't know the truth.

She kept her head lowered and focused on her hands clenched on her lap. Two worn, but clean black leather boots appeared in her field of vision. Her heart sped up and beat so loud in her ears it nearly drowned out the hushed murmurs of the gossipy town. A familiar low drawl blanketed her as she stared at his boots. "Hello, Kendall."

Damian. Her heart stopped for a moment as his familiar deep growl rolled over her and rattled around in her chest.

Kendall slowly drew her gaze up his long legs and trim

waist, over the dress shirt she knew covered tight muscles honed from years of brutal physical ranch work and a regular regimen of weights and running, and up to that gorgeous, sun-kissed face. Damian Sloane had been an attractive if gangly young man when she'd last seen him four years before. But now he was a man, a man with his black hair just a little too long…almost like he couldn't be bothered with a haircut and at least a week's growth of dark beard that did nothing to hide those angular cheekbones and intense hazel eyes that sometimes glowed green at the edges.

She took a deep centering breath like those meditation videos on the Internet instructed.

"Hello, Damian." Probably best to keep it simple and not start off with why she'd snuck out on him all those years ago and where she'd been since. Even if he did know, he probably wouldn't care at this point. Too much water under that bridge.

He held his hat his in hands and gestured to the empty spot next to her. "Mind if I sit?" She did. Of course she did, because the truth was that Damian Sloane drove her mad. Mad with rage, mad with hurt, but mostly mad with longing. She was already strung tighter than a taut guitar string and having him next to her throughout the entire service would surely send her over the edge. Instead of protesting, though, she nodded. She was determined to not have the fight that had been brewing between them for years blow up in front of the town. She'd had enough public humiliation to last a lifetime and wasn't eager for anymore, *thankyouvery-much.*

Damian bent his tall, muscled frame and sat beside her, setting his hat on the other side of him. Instead of putting space between them like she desperately needed, he pressed his leg up against hers. Fire seemed to burn from the spot their legs touched and spread through her body like lava. Her breath hitched and then completely stopped for a moment when he angled slightly toward her body and placed his hand on her knee, the one still wearing the thick gold band she'd put on his finger years ago. A cruel smile formed on his lips before he reached over with his other hand and gripped her chin with his long, tanned fingers. Pulling her face to his he rubbed his lips across hers roughly and pulled back slightly so he could peer down at her.

"Welcome home, wife." In that moment, all the hurt, all the anger, and all the betrayal of young love came rushing back like a bullet train, every flashing window a single memory ripped from the past she tried so hard to keep down. Of all the things she'd imagined happening on this day, him kissing and laying claim to her once again in front of the whole town was not part of it.

As he smirked and leaned back against the pew with his huge hand still resting on her knee, Kendall realized what she had forgotten so long ago. Damian Sloane was more danger-ous than any con artist musician she'd met on the road and could be meaner than any rattlesnake. But, more importantly, he'd never actually given her heart back.

"AND THE OTHER fifty percent of said property is hereby willed to Damian Sloane," Joe McGreevy repeated for the third time before closing the brown folder he read from. He, Kendall, and Damian sat in Joe's stately office with its gray walls and dark wood desk and built-in shelving lined with impressive legal tomes, looking more like a city firm and not so much a small-town lawyer and partner. It was designed to intimidate.

Damian hid the vengeful smile threatening to break free and left the taunting words he wanted to spit at Kendall sitting on his tongue. The look on her beautiful face was satisfying enough without showing his hand by out-and-out gloating. How did she still look so stunning after the wringer the press had put her through and, even now, learning that what she considered hers was in actual fact only half hers? She flipped her long pink and blonde braid back over her shoulder and flashed him a look brimming with controlled rage before turning back to her grandmother's attorney and Damian's dad's partner.

"I understood the first time you read it, Mr. McGreevy. What I don't understand is how she could do this. And, more importantly, how do I get it reversed?" Kendall's voice didn't betray her anger or frustration, which Damian found more than a little interesting. And slightly frustrating. His Kendall couldn't keep a secret or hide an emotion to save her life. But she wasn't his Kendall, was she? No, she'd given up that title four years ago when she'd left him in the middle of the night. And he wanted her to suffer...like he had. But how to do that when he was tied to her through the Kelly Family Farms?

"There is no realistic recourse, Ms. Kelly. The will is on solid legal ground," Joe said standing and signaling the end of the meeting.

"But...but what about contesting the will?" Kendall sputtered and kept her seat, not ready to give up the fight, always prepared to go toe-to-toe and do battle. Damian stood, because he was ready for this part of the dog and pony show to be over. Time to move to the next stage.

"That's within your legal rights, certainly. However, you'll have to prove duress or undue influence or whatever your protest is. And, frankly, Ms. Kelly, you've been gone a long time and it could work against you especially since Mr. Sloane has not only resided on the property in your absence, he's maintained it and grown a business there as well." Joe's pinched face was more rat-like than usual, and almost gleeful. Clearly, he was enjoying Kendall's misery. And that should please Damian, because he was, too. However, Damian had every reason to want Kendall to be unhappy and Joe had no justification for taking pleasure in her losing half of what she considered her birthright. And being the selfish dick he was, Damian wanted to own all her misery.

"The courts could find you remiss and void the entire will. It could go into probate, or be tied up in the court system for years." Joe maneuvered around the desk and held out his hand for Damian to shake.

"Congratulations on your new property, Damian," Joe said smugly and turned to Kendall who had reluctantly realized the meeting was over and stood. "I'm sure you'll work it out with Ms. Kelly. And if you both decide to sell the property, I could find the time in my schedule to represent you as larger parcels of land can be tricky and might require legal input."

Kendall didn't hide her surprise and interest at the seemingly bizarre, out-of-nowhere comment, but this wasn't the first time Damian had heard it. In fact, his dad had emailed him occasionally over the last few years with that same suggestion—talk Mary Ellen into selling the farm, make a mint, go back to school. Which, of course, meant he and Joe had an agenda when it came to the Kelly—well, now the Kelly and Sloane—property. An agenda that probably included a developer with a large checkbook.

Thanks, but no thanks.

Damian ignored Joe and held the door open for Kendall who stomped out in that slinky dress that stuck to her hips like plastic wrap and those silly rhinestone boots that he longed to feel wrapped around his ass just one more time. Hot as fuck, that woman. Too bad she was an untrustworthy two-timing runaway wife. And despite all the rage making his skin feel swollen and tight, it was still almost a reflex to reach out and run his finger down her arm. He didn't. But he wanted to goddammit.

As Damian suspected, his dad was leaning against a paralegal's desk outside the office wearing a custom-tailored suit and subtle gray silk tie—the very same uniform Jonathan Sloane had worn nearly his entire life.

"Damian," his father greeted. "You're looking well. I'm sure your mother would appreciate a visit or call from you." No pretense, just straight into his dearest dad act.

"What about you, Dad? Would you enjoy a call or visit too? Or just Mom?" There was no use being civil with his father. He never responded well to civility; only hostility seemed to breach that cold layer of ice around the elder Sloane.

"Your attitude is beneath you, son. I was merely suggesting a family dinner or even a call." His father, who was still a handsome man with a full head of gray hair he kept short and styled, tugged his cuffs and straightened to his full height. Unfortunately for Jon Sloane he came up a couple inches shorter than his son.

"And my wife? Is she invited to this little reunion, too?" Damian asked, suddenly protective of the woman who had shredded his heart to ribbons years ago. Reaching for her hand against his better judgment and the very loud red-flag warnings sounding in his head, he pulled her down the hall without bothering to wait for a response. It was always the same with his father—control the message, manage his family, and be the richest guy in town. None of those goals appealed to Damian on any level.

When they'd made it to the parking lot, Kendall yanked her hand from his. "What was that, Damian?" She fumed while rifling through her purse, most likely for the keys to her rental car. She yanked them out and threw the car door open and turned to him. Her face was the gut punch he was never prepared for. Yes, she was beautiful, but it was more, something else entirely, that made him hurt when he looked at her. Something wrapped in their shared history, the plans they'd made and the love they'd had. She had belonged to him once—he'd known that deep in his bones—and then she'd defied all logic and walked out on him for a music career that she claimed she never wanted. He'd never even known how badly she craved the spotlight having only ever shown a hobbyist's interest in singing at home and some-times in town.

"Are you listening to me?" Her voice was stretched tight, thinning and ready to snap. "I want my farm back and I'm not your wife anymore." Her voice shook with fury and her pale skin was turning red. Tough shit. He was pissed, too. At her. At this life she'd left him in alone years ago.

"It's only half your farm now, Kendall. And you're still my wife and unless you plan on staying married to me I suggest you cut the attitude and stop acting like a petulant, wounded child. Obviously we have a lot to discuss."

"Funny, you sound just like your father," she said and threw herself into her car and drove off without a glance back.

KENDALL KELLY HAD finally come home.

Damian Sloane watched the trail of billowing dust behind her rental car as it flew up the long gravel and dirt driveway toward the farmhouse. The darkening shadows and the setting sun made it too difficult to see the driver's face, but he knew who it was. He pulled the tractor into the barn for the night and turned off the motor. The familiar smells of wood, mud, and hay surrounded him. Jumping from the seat he cursed to himself.

He hadn't known if she would come back here after their altercation in the parking lot. In fact, after a couple of hours of looking out for her car he figured she'd found a place to stay in town.

Kendall. Wearer of rhinestones, singer of songs, and breaker of hearts. His being just the first of many a very long time ago.

He pulled the heavy steel doors shut on the newly constructed barn and punched in the security code to lock it up. Gravel crunched under his work boots and acid churned in his gut as he slowly walked up the path to the dark house.

Frogs croaked and bugs sang as night settled over the farm. Pops of light broke through the windows of the weary old farmhouse as she worked her way from room to room. Stepping up the creaky steps and over the porch he suddenly felt almost as old as the house itself, which had stood for nearly one hundred years on that same spot, supposedly built as a labor of love for Kendall's great-grandmother by her great-grandfather when they'd bought the property years after emigrating from Ireland.

He waited in the entry until she stomped downstairs again and stopped abruptly.

"Damian." Her voice was soft, with that smoky undertone that had made her a star. It was that same voice that kept him away during her previous visits because it chipped away at his resolve to forget their complicated past, to stay firm in his anger. The same voice that sucked the air from his lungs and made it impossible to breathe. Or speak, for that matter.

"Kendall." He pulled the hat off his head and held it in his hands as he willed the air back into his lungs. "I should have called you about your grandmother and the will," Damian said.

And he really should have. He'd meant to...even picked up his phone and punched in the number Sabre had texted him before she'd died. But then the numbness, the cold who-gives-a-fuck lack of emotion he'd attached to Kendall the Star would melt away and all his goddamn feelings would flood back. The ache and the longing would boil up to the top again and then the anger. The inferno in his belly would spread everywhere and take over every calm, rational thought.

Kendall had turned her back on him and what was left of her family the night she'd snuck out of town and hitchhiked to Los Angeles. Sure, he knew she'd come back a handful of times to visit her grandmother, but she usually slipped in late at night when she knew he'd be tucked into the little cottage he'd called home since graduating from high school, and she was gone by morning. She came whenever the old woman had called, probably still holding out hope that her grandmother would show her some semblance of affection or familial love. She never stayed long enough to give him an explanation or even the middle finger. She just didn't care enough about her old life to give up any part of her new one.

For the first year, he'd written to her and called until she'd changed her number and his letters started coming back unopened. He'd even gone down to Los Angeles to try and find out what happened, bring her home if he could. But she'd been so bright and comfortable on the stage already that he knew it wasn't his place to interfere with fate. Problem was he thought they had been destined to be together.

So he tried to not give a shit. Tried to be callous and move on like she apparently had, but it had been nearly impossible. How did one move on from their first—their only—love? Lord knows he'd tried with other women. None of them stuck. None of them dug under his skin and stayed there. None of them even made it past the first, chaste date. Only one. Kendall. He'd learned to live with the bitter, grizzled version of himself he'd become. Soon enough it had stopped feeling achy and uncomfortable. Soon enough it began to wear on him, not in a bad way, but more like an old torn-up pair of boots. Worn in and expected. Almost easy.

After he'd impulsively kissed her yesterday and put his hand on her knee for the entire service, he'd wondered if maybe one more time in his bed would finally work her out of his system, turn his bitterness to acceptance. Maybe he could prove she was the devious schemer he knew she was and he could finally move the hell on.

He hung his hat on the dusty rack near the door and crossed his arms against his chest, holding his ground.

She tapped her chipped glittery nail on her bracelet, a habit she'd always had even when she was just a cute little girl begging for a ride on his horse. "Now what?"

"Well, sweetheart, you heard the lawyer. You move in or, if you want out, you buy me out. Should be a fairly simple transaction for a big star like yourself."

Her pale skin turned pink. Her short temper was a thing of beauty and his dark side yearned to set fire it to it again. "First off, you're my husband in name only. You don't deserve even one mud cake of this dirt pile. Second, this is not my home. It never was. You and everyone else have made that perfectly clear." She kept her hands at her sides, but her fists were balls of creeping rage, white at the knuckles and rolled tight into her palms. But if he looked closely, and he always did look closely when it came to Kendall, he could see the hard points of her nipples through the material of her thin dress and what he knew must be a sheer lacy bra. "But…" she said slowly "…if you'd just agree to sell then we could both move on."

He took a step toward her. "Damian," she warned and took a step backward toward the wall. "Please." Her voice lowered; her expression was almost one of panic. From anger to fear to lust—that was Kendall. One big ball of passion.

"I'm not selling." He took another step bringing him to within inches of her body. The air around them vibrated with energy, something dark and volatile, yet familiar. Unused lightning in the storm they always seemed to create together. Her moist lips parted and he could hear her slight intake of breath. Good. She should suffer this ache as he had for the last four years.

Hooded sparkling brown eyes looked up into his. "Why, Damian, why won't you let us move on?" Her voice was hoarse, barely a whisper in the quiet evening of the darkening house, and barely recognizable from the husky drawl that had made her famous.

"I'm trying." And for a second, for some ridiculous reason he couldn't fathom and really didn't care to examine, he wanted to reach out and smooth his hand down her now pink-and-blonde-streaked hair, and it wasn't because of the way she used to smile up at him when he'd do that. It wasn't because of the weary stare behind her eyes that he hadn't noticed earlier. It wasn't even because he wanted to gather her full mop in his fist and tug it under his kiss. It wasn't for any of those reasons. It was because no matter how selfish and heartless she was, he knew she was grieving—for her sister, for her grandma, for her career, and now for her family home. He knew this unfinished thing that sparked between them terrified her. And he knew she'd lost the only two remaining members in her family in under a year. He was a dick for messing with her. But he couldn't help himself. It had been years since he'd had her this close and the opportunity was just too good.

Kendall shook her head in answer to all the unaddressed questions between them. Her eyes glistened with unshed tears and she took a visibly deep breath, gulping air down like she was starving for it. "You're not. Just let me go. We both know you don't want me. And I don't want you."

But suddenly he knew that was a lie. The hitch in her breath, the pink tongue darting out to slide across her bottom lip, and the slight tremble of her body were her tells. Finally, he reached up and smoothed his hand over her hair, gathering the length of the braid in his hand and tugging her head back. "Liar," he whispered and lowered his lips to hers. He'd intended to play with her. Kiss her dismissively like he had in the church. Instead, a plan began to form in his head. She would stay for a while and eventually he'd buy her out. Divorce her. Let her go like she said she wanted.

But now, he'd take his fill. He devoured her, parting her lips with his tongue, reminding her that this time she'd leave knowing who she belonged to. This time she would leave with the image of his tongue in her mouth and his sex in hers. This time, he would screw her out of his system and he wouldn't be left with his bleeding heart in his hands. When she left this time, it would truly be over between them.

Chapter Two

WHEN DAMIAN'S MOUTH crashed down onto hers the pointless thought that she should push him away and run from the old creaky house flitted through her mind. But his hand was wrapped in her hair and his other hand, fingers worn and calloused from years of hard work, had come up to caress her jaw and his body caged her in against the hall wall. He was so warm, and his kiss felt like home. What could it possibly hurt to let him hold her for a minute? He was still her husband after all.

So instead of running away—which, let's face it, was her modus operandi—she melted into his long body, feeling the pressure of his erection pressed into her belly through the denim of his jeans. She heard a low groan and quickly realized it came from her. Of course it did, everything Damian did was so controlled, so calculated. She longed to make him lose control like she once had, watch as his rigid demeanor peeled away from him like so much discarded clothing.

Without thought, she yanked his T-shirt from his jeans. She nearly stopped breathing when her hands met with his hard, hot body underneath. She spread her fingers on his concrete back, noting every line and divot, like he was a map. A really sexy, really hard map. He was so much bigger, stronger than he had been before. Damian had always been ripped, but this was ridiculous. She ran her hands around to his front down his chest, finding a light smattering of rough hair under her hands that had grown thicker, and then down to his defined abs.

God, this man's body. It was so much…more than any other. Not that she had carnal knowledge of any other man or his body. Quite the opposite. She had tried. But despite celebrity news reports to the contrary, including the much-covered "relationship" gone wrong with her criminal of a business manager, no other man could make it past the first grope before she ended it. That and the endless work to succeed had never provided the adequate time or motivation to try for more with anyone.

There was only Damian. There had only ever been him from the time she was a child until their wedding night when he'd kissed her so much differently than he was now. That night when she'd finally shared herself with him, and him with her. So long ago. A beautiful memory erased by so much betrayal, so much pain. And a giant lie.

His hand left her hair and pushed aside part of her dress, exposing her black lace bra and her breast, her traitorous nipple tightening to an almost painful point. While his other hand slid up her body, tracing her curves until he cupped both her breasts. "God, your body. I missed your sweet, tight nipples," he said, his voice thin like the admission hurt to say. He pinched one bud with his forefinger and thumb, much too hard but not hard enough, sending spikes of desire through her entire body while his other hand made the long trek back down her torso, slowly…achingly.

Finally his hand peeked under the hem of her dress and crept up her thigh. Kendall should probably be embarrassed by the moisture slicking the inside of her legs, especially since this possessed man was not really her husband any longer, was not the man who'd gently taken her virginity as a gift on her wedding night. This man was clearly out to punish her with his lust, make her pay for leaving him. But she refused to feel anything but her own desire. Their love might be no more, but their sexual heat had clearly never burned away.

Widening her legs, she felt two blunt, work-rough fingers stroke the outside of her panties. Again, too much and not quite enough. She leaned in to his hand, needing more, and heard his dark chuckle just before he tugged her thong aside and parted her folds. She felt her pulse beat frantically, battering her ribs, just as he bit down on that place that drove her crazy, that sensitive spot at the base of her neck. She hated him for being the only person in the world to know all her buttons, hated him for so much more.

His calloused fingers breached her body and suddenly there was no air. It had been sucked out of the room, probably out of the damn house, by his heat. His fire must demand all the oxygen within a ten-mile radius in order to burn so fierce. And there was nothing else anywhere that mattered. Just Damian. And his command of her body.

He wrapped his bulging arm around her waist and pushed her up against the wall, forcing her legs around his lean hips with his fingers still inside her body, his thumb circling her clit. In the back of her mind she knew he wasn't her safe place. Hell, she didn't believe in such things anymore, but for that moment she wanted to pretend he was. His warm breath caressed her as his fingers pistoned in and out of her and his thumb began to circle the tightened bundle of nerves of her clit.

"Come for me, baby." His harsh whisper was all it took for her to spiral into the abyss, shattered and ruined, where nothing else existed but him and her and this unquenchable fire they seemed to always create. Kendall finally took in a deep breath, followed by another, until she felt herself slowly float back. Behind her closed eyelids, lights still blazed bright and her pulse was ragged. A harsh, warm breath in her ear snapped her back to where she was. In the only real childhood home she knew. After burying the last member of her family.

"This can't happen. This didn't happen." Her voice, even to her, sounded strained, breathless.

"It just did, sweetheart. Welcome home," Damian said, bitterness bleeding from his words. "Figure your shit out. I'll be back for you in two hours." He pushed off the wall and away from her.

Still gasping for air, she shoved her hand to her hip. "What does that even mean? Back for what?"

He was already halfway out the front door with his hat in his hand when he turned and raked his gaze over her from head to toe.

"I can't stay here, Damian," she said, disappointed at the pleading tone in her voice. "I want to sell this place and I want you to sign the divorce papers." She didn't add that it was more need than want that drove her. She needed to pay back the money her business manager had embezzled from her, the advance money the record label was demanding be repaid. Even though what she really wanted was to go back in time. To fix the past. But that wasn't possible. He still would have chosen Blackberry Cove and she still would have had to leave.

"Need and want are two different things, Kendall. This is your home."

"No, honey, this is just the place I'm from," she snapped.

He didn't rise to the bait. Didn't fight back or try to soothe her temper like he'd always done. Damian smiled, that enigmatic thing he did curving one side of his mouth that had panties dropping across three counties. "Like I said. Straighten your shit out. I'll be back after my work is done and then we're gonna talk."

The giant cinder block that had been sitting on her chest all day slipped down into her gut. She needed that money and she needed to get out of this town before she lost what little sanity she had left.

"I'll be gone by then. And I'll be back with my lawyer."

He laughed, a deep hollow sound that unfurled something prickly and uncomfortable in her chest and set his black cowboy hat on his head. "No, you won't," he said, turning and leaving her standing in the dark entryway.

Silently she slid down the wall, pulled her knees into her chest, and sobbed fat wet tears into her hands.

DAMIAN GLANCED AT the antique clock on his mantel again. Time to go hash it out with Kendall. At first, before he'd shoved her against the wall and coaxed an orgasm from her, he'd planned on figuring out how to buy her out and get her back on her merry, backstabbing way. But that was before. Before he'd touched her silky skin again, before he'd seen something float past her ironclad armor that looked a lot like regret, before he'd seen the tears leak from the corners of her eyes as he sent her over the edge.

Before all that.

He'd finished up the farm chores and consulted with his crew on their orders for the following week. Then he'd marched off to his little cabin in the tree grove, back behind the main house, and paced. Still, he had nothing. No idea what his plan was. Because now he wasn't just angry and bitter—the two emotions that pushed him out of bed every morning before sunrise and kept him working until after dark—now he felt something else. And he couldn't quite figure out just what the hell it was.

And that made him even angrier. Which, of course, made no more sense than pushing her up against the wall and having his way with her.

Maybe he wanted her to suffer a little, shake her up. She seemed so different from the old Kendall, the girl who displayed every emotion on her face like a neon sign. In the last few years, other than the one time he'd flown to Los Angeles to see her open for a big-name pop star, he'd only seen her in the media or the Internet. At first, she'd been so composed, so obviously trained by some public relations expert to act and talk a certain way. But in the last year she'd begun to publicly unravel. Stress lines around her mouth and eyes began to morph into reckless behavior played out for the world to watch, like a car wreck you couldn't take your eyes from.

In just a few months, Kendall Kelly the punk rock cowgirl, had gone from celebrated crossover artist to tabloid fodder. And, man, had the press been vicious. How they loved to tear down someone they'd helped build up.

Now she was here, his runaway wife, asking him to buy her out of the farm and sign the divorce papers. He glanced down at his desk, glaring at the folder containing those damned documents. Why hadn't he signed them yet? He'd wanted to carve her from his mind for so long. But now he had the ability to do that and he couldn't quite pull the trigger.

Why?

Not because he still loved her, that was for fucking sure. And not because he held out some ridiculously romantic notion that she was still the one when she clearly wasn't. Moving to the door and grabbing his hat before he moved out onto his deck, he looked out on the watercolor horizon and took a deep breath. The purple- and pink-tinged clouds hung along the mountain backdrop, highlighting the green treetops growing dark with the thinning light.

God, he loved this place. Loved it with all that was left of his shattered heart. Why couldn't she have been happy here? With him? Maybe he was the problem and not Blackberry Cove?

His eyes dropped to the back porch of the main house across the wide yard from his smaller cottage as the screen door slammed and the silhouette of a woman, an angry woman, barreled toward him.

He wouldn't have to go to her this time. Taking a moment to admire her deliberate step and the long pink braid flying behind her, he noticed she'd changed from her dress to a pair of old loose jeans and a fitted plaid shirt. For a moment, he was reminded of the day they'd run off and gotten married in Las Vegas. Her eighteenth birthday. They'd been so young and though he was only a few years older, he felt like he'd been waiting forever for her. That day she'd skipped from the main house to his smaller guesthouse and jumped into his arms. She'd kissed the side of his neck and said, "Let's go get married, cowboy." And they had been happy for a while. Before she'd ripped out his heart and run off to Los Angeles. Before she'd become a star and then a national laughing stock.

"Damian," she yelled just before hitting his deck. "I'm ready to talk now." Her pink cheeks practically vibrated with rage.

Tough. He sat down on his old Adirondack chair and gestured to the swing across from him, the swing they'd had their first kiss on. "Talk then."

Kendall crossed her legs primly, if a little awkwardly, on the old, unstable swing and smoothed her hands over her hair before clasping them tightly in her lap.

"I need you to buy me out. And I need you to sign the papers." She took a deep breath and then with a look reminiscent of the old Kendall she added, "*Please*, Damian."

"As much as I'd like you to be gone, I can't buy you out. Not yet anyway."

"Why not yet?"

"Have you bothered to look around? Kelly Family Farms is a working farm...a *profitable* working farm. We have a healthy CSA business going, as well as goat milk products...a whole bath and body line we sell locally and online. This isn't the same dirt patch you ran away from, Kendall."

Awareness lit her face as she looked around. It was getting too dark to see much, and most of the crew had already left. They'd been on short staff and even shorter hours due to the memorial, but she could see well enough that the landscape of the farm had changed. Transformed. She would see the condition of his cottage had altered drastically since she'd left, that it was nearly twice as big and a dozen times nicer.

"I didn't know," she answered quietly as she ran her foot over the stained wood of the deck. "The cottage…"

"We got a loan. Made some investments in equipment, built a new barn, bought some goats, hired staff."

When he mentioned the goats she tried to hide her smile by ducking her head, but he saw it nonetheless. For a moment, it softened his jagged edges, made him not hate her. So much. Took him back to the afternoon they'd sat on this very porch and made plans for the farm. Kendall had strummed her guitar while they talked about their future, their plan for the farm once her grandmother gave them a stake in it. Kendall had wanted goats even back then and he'd laughed, teasing her that she'd be a big country music star one day. She denied it, and made him promise that one day they'd have a whole bunch of them. "Goats," she said quietly.

"Yeah."

They sat quietly for several minutes while she looked over his shoulder as the sun made its dramatic exit and the sky began to fill with stars. He never tired of how bright the stars were out here in the country.

"If you got a loan then why can't you buy me out? You don't want me here, Damian. I know you don't. And I don't belong here."

He sighed, probably a little more dramatically than he'd meant to. "That's not it. I just made a bulk loan payment and until some of our receivables come due and we sell off some of our inventory I won't be in a position to buy you out."

"How long?"

"What's the hurry, Kendall?" he asked, taunting her.

"You've seen the news?" He nodded, and she looked into her lap at her hands twisted tightly together. What he wouldn't do to erase the tension she held like a trophy. Having her trembling in his arms earlier that day had released him from his own angst and the memories of love lost for just a little while.

"It's worse than that." She looked up into his eyes. The light had come on over his door, bathing the porch in a soft glow. Without the makeup she'd had on earlier, he could suddenly see the dark circles under her eyes. And more…more sadness than he'd seen etched on her beautiful face *ever*. Why was his default to comfort her even after she was solely responsible for his misery the last four years?

"How?"

"I owe my label because I pulled out of my last recording project. But I don't have the money. My business manager took it…mismanaged everything. Contractually I'm responsible though. I have to pay it back."

Jumping up from his chair, a wave of irrational rage broke over him. That was the last jackass she'd been with. At least, that's what the tabloids had reported. In less than two strides he reached her. He wanted to put his hands on her shoulders, shake her, get the asshole's name and beat him to a pulp. Instead he fisted his hands at his sides. "Well, make your jerkoff of a business manager pay it back."

"I can't. No one can find him. I wasn't the only one he screwed. Figuratively, of course."

Of course. Well, no, not of course. She had had well-publicized liaisons with actors and other musicians since she'd been gone even though she'd technically been married to him. How the hell could he know what was real and what wasn't? So over the years he'd just tortured himself and assumed they were all true.

Pacing back across the porch, he wondered how smart it was to have her around the farm now. His Helen of Troy. But what could it hurt for her to stick around for a while? Punish her for her betrayal? She could do some real work for once and, at the same time, hide from the press until the drama of her implosion became just another story.

"Why don't you just make the record?"

Kendall lifted her shoulder. "My last one didn't sell that well, to be honest. And…my heart's just not in it anymore."

Damian didn't know what to do with her admission.

Did that mean she'd left him, their marriage, for a career that she'd lost interest in? Or did it mean something else altogether?

"Stay. For a few weeks. Get away from the tabloids. You can help me work the farm, get your grandmother's house purged and updated, and then I'll buy you out. You can move on to where ever it is you're going next." For reasons he wasn't ready to define, Damian found himself hoping she'd say yes. Hoping she'd stay and maybe they could find some kind of peace between them before she moved on again. And this time it would be over for good and he could take his life back.

She stared out at the horizon as the last hue of pink disappeared into the darkness behind the hills. The entire time she tapped her bracelet. Thinking, thinking, thinking. Or, in Kendall's case, probably overthinking. Because that was her way. She always used to say that he was her quiet place, that he helped slow the chaos in her head. But that had been a long time ago. The job was no longer his.

"Okay." But she didn't smile when she looked up at him, though she somberly nodded before walking back toward the main house.

Chapter Three

I T'S A WELL-KNOWN fact that the lifestyle of a rock star by definition is not conducive to early mornings as it usually entails a lot of late nights and even more sleeping in. Unfortunately for Kendall, a farmer's lifestyle entails just the opposite: early mornings followed by a boatload of hard work. By the time she'd made her way back to her grandmother's house the night before and then cleaned up her old room well enough to sleep in, it had been past midnight. Which is why it hurt to peel her eyes open at—she peered over at the clock—five in the morning.

"It's Sunday," she croaked to the blurry form of a man standing over her. "And you're in my bedroom."

"I am still your husband," he said sternly but she sensed the amusement in his tone. "And this is a twenty-four-hour, year-round working farm, sweetheart. Get your ass up and let's get to work."

"Ugh," she groaned and pulled the sheet back over her head. Her eyes flew open when cold air hit her body like a sheet of ice. Damian stood above her clutching the sheet in his hand, his eyes wide staring at her body with undisguised want in his eyes. Suddenly he dropped the material and dragged his hand down his jaw.

"Jesus, Kendall." His face colored and his eyes turned dark before he forcibly closed them and turned his back to her.

It had been so long since anybody had made her feel like an attractive woman. Sure, men hit on her constantly, but she was either a trophy to them or just another notch on the old belt. Damian looked at her with a dirty kind of reverence laced with just a bit of pain. And that giant hole inside her chest pulsed with…want or need or regret. Or all of the above. Damian hated her for the way she'd left and never looked back, but she couldn't help craving the way his gaze ate at her and the way he made her body throb. She liked it. She liked it a lot.

"Prude. It's not like I'm naked." She bit back a laugh as she sat up.

"No, but your tiny nightshirt doesn't leave much to the imagination. I'm trying to be a gentleman."

She laughed as she threw on a pair of old jeans and a sweatshirt. "Oh really? Since when? Besides I'm decent now." She wasn't ready to bring up their interlude in the entryway the day before. Damian turned slowly, his eyes burning across her body, burning her raw from the outside in.

"I need to freshen up, wash my face, and I'll meet you downstairs in fifteen minutes." Yeah, she was exhausted, but she wasn't letting him get under her skin. She needed to send some emails and get the snarling pack of wolves off her back. But she'd get to those that evening. And once that was done, she'd do her time on the farm and get the hell out.

And go where?

Well, where didn't matter. Anywhere but Blackberry Cove and over one hundred miles away from Damian Sloane was the correct answer. Because for the first time since her early childhood she didn't know what the next step would be. When she was little she went where her mother dragged her, from one man to the next until she'd been left on Nana's broken old deck. Shortly after that she met Delilah and they had each other.

Around that same time she'd discovered an old acoustic guitar and some classic country sheet music in some forgotten corner of the attic. She'd carefully dusted the grime off the instrument and taught herself those songs from videos on the Internet. The music had been her salvation, her entertainment, and her gift. She improved so quickly Nana had stopped belittling her when she played and was, for once, thankfully silent. Making music changed everything. Not in any obvious way. Music created its magic inside of her. Made her feel taller, prettier, smarter. And not so lonely.

Then Damian had turned her entire world upside down and inside out. She'd learned how to trust and love another human being without the fear of hurt or loss. Even after she'd left him she'd known what direction she was headed.

Now that her music career was over and she had no interest in living in that hellacious machine that chewed up people like her, she had no idea what was next. There probably weren't a lot of bands willing to take on singer songwriter guitar players with a reputation for not paying her musicians, not to mention her abysmal image in the press. When she'd left Damian that night so many years ago she'd gotten a bus ticket for LA only because she figured she'd be able to land a job as a waitress easily. The bar she'd landed at let her play her guitar when the crowd was thin so she could earn a few dollars in tips. It had just happened. She'd never sought it, never earned it. And embarrassing as it was, she'd never wanted it.

A life with her husband on this farm had been her dream all along. But that hadn't been the hand she'd been dealt. So she'd take what she could get, she'd focus on these few weeks on this property, with Damian. She'd stay back-breakingly busy and lose herself in the work, the feel of the dirt in her hands.

Kendall quickly completed her business and pulled her hair into a single, messy braid, making it downstairs in under fifteen minutes.

Take that, bossy man.

Damian was standing with his back to her, staring out the big kitchen window, with a halo of soft light outlining his broad body. He wore a thick flannel shirt over a hooded sweatshirt and his black weathered hat sat low on his head. A familiar ache settled into her bones as she grabbed a cup of coffee and added some cream before joining him. The sky was still dark, but the edge of the sun peeked over the rolling hills bordering the eastern half of the property, and a rooster was already crowing because a working farm never waited until daylight for the day to begin. Though it had been years since she'd sent him off to work the farm early in the morning, his silhouette invoked an intimacy so innate she nearly reached for him, but she held on to her cup and shoved her other hand in her jeans pocket.

"So what's our plan?" she asked, looking up at his strong jawline, the one she could still see through his trimmed beard. There was no denying Damian Sloane was a very good-looking man. The last few years had taken his boyish handsomeness and morphed it into something a little harder, a lot tougher than he'd been, but ruthlessly beautiful nevertheless. In fact, of all the men she'd met in LA, none could hold a candle to his rugged cowboy looks.

Without turning, he spoke. "We have a shorter chore list on Sundays. Usually have a couple hands to help out, but I gave them the rest of the weekend off. We need to feed and milk the goats, hose down the milking stations, and check on the gardens, as well as check on the hens and gather eggs. Normally I'd take more time to show you around, but I have a date tonight. We'll do the full tour tomorrow."

That heavy weight in her chest dropped to her belly. He had a date. Because he had a life now that didn't include her. Maybe one that included a girlfriend. She'd chosen that for both of them, but still couldn't ignore the stab of discomfort between her ribs. She'd only run from him because she'd had to, not because she'd suddenly stopped loving him or had an insatiable need to play music on a big stage. She'd run because he was going to give up his family, his life for her, because she couldn't give him the family they'd promised each other. And she couldn't do that to him. Not then and not now.

She swallowed down the weird little jab, she swallowed down the past, and she swallowed down any feelings about how he'd touched her the evening before and simply nodded. As she turned to set her cup in the sink a huge whitish beige bundle of fur ran in through the back door and bounded into the kitchen, landing in front of two large steel bowls full of food and water she hadn't noticed. Jumping back to prevent being trampled she screeched. "What the hell is that? A bear?"

The curve of Damian's mouth made her want to forget everything she'd resolved to not do and jump into his arms. "Dog. Shrek." He laughed. "He was supposed to be herd protection…stay outside and protect the goats, but he decided he wanted to be a pet. I had to get another animal for the night watch."

Her racing heart slowed, and she stared at the giant animal wolfing its food down, before it suddenly ran to her and smothered her hand in slobber. She patted it on the head. "Nice dog."

"For a country girl, you sure are skittish around animals."

She rolled her eyes. "Whatever. Let's go, cowboy." What Damian didn't realize was that Kendall craved the oblivion that physical work provided. She was looking forward to the kind of hard work that would help her perhaps forget about the clouds of doom floating above her head. Maybe she'd even forget the constant empty ache in her chest she felt every time she looked over at the man she was supposed to spend forever with.

Damian handed her a pair of oversized gloves and led her out to the goat pen and animal barn. When Damian unlatched the gate, a flood of goats of different ages and colors scattered out followed by a gray donkey with a decidedly arrogant expression.

"So, a donkey?" she asked.

"Herd protection." He raised a brow in answer and swept his arm toward the animals.

"Seriously?" In the dusky morning light, she was fascinated by the goats' funny little sounds, and prancing, playful demeanor. The donkey stood guard over them, walking back and forth but never far from the herd even when he finally dipped his head into his trough to eat. For a moment all she could do was clap her gloved hands together and laugh at their antics. When she looked up her laughter caught in her throat as her gaze snagged on his—intense hazel eyes stripping her bare and leaving her exposed.

"What's his name?" she asked more to cover the ugly throbbing hole in her chest than from real interest.

"Donkey," he said and that one corner of his mouth turned up reminding her of an unspoken dirty vow.

Dammit. How was she ever going to make it through the next few weeks or however long it took to get him to buy her out when he looked at her like that...a terrifyingly potent mix of amusement and longing on his face before it turned hard, cold, unforgiving? Shaking off the chill he'd suddenly directed at her, Kendall smiled. She would let their shattered past dictate her reactions from now on, she reassured herself. She would not get caught up in Damian's warm eyes or wish he'd wrap her in his big arms just one more time. She would stay like she promised and then she would leave. This time for good. It was best that way.

For him, anyway.

No LONGER COATED in goat shit and mud, Damian stepped from the shower, toweled himself off, and began to dress for his date with Carissa. He'd dodged the mayor's daughter and her overt advances for years. Back in his senior year of high school she'd even gone so far as to ambush him naked at a party, and if it had been even a month before, he probably would have taken her up on her blatant offer. She was pretty and smart. But a few weeks before he'd seen something that would change his life forever.

Kendall Kelly. One very hot afternoon that year, just days before school let out for the summer and he would be preparing to go off to university to study political science and then law, he'd seen her sitting under the shade of an old oak tree strumming on a battered guitar. Her long blonde hair had been blowing around her face and he could see the freckles dancing across the bridge of her nose even from where he stood on the walkway several feet away.

Sure he'd known her since she was little; everyone knew the Kellys' granddaughter. She'd been dropped off at her grandmother's by her mother at the age of ten and had forevermore been known as Poor Little Kendall Kelly. At least until she'd swanned out of town four years before and shown up on television and in the tabloids as that year's newest it-girl, the punk rock cowgirl. With the brash, brazen style of a rocker and the sweet, dulcet voice of a country singer from back in the day. Damian had been the only one in town not surprised at Kendall's talent and popularity, as he'd been the only one, including her own grandma, who hadn't written her off as basic expendable trash.

Until Kendall had taken off, he'd never even looked at another girl or woman. Was never even tempted. Instead of leaving town for the school his family had picked for him, he'd opted to study agricultural science at the local college so he could stay close to Kendall. Mary Ellen had traded him work for lodging and he'd patiently waited for Kendall to graduate high school before he went against his family's wishes and ran off to Vegas for an Elvis-officiated wedding. He'd been so sure she was his one and only. Sure enough to allow his family to disown him and move into that crappy cottage. He'd forgone the carefully planned future his parents had crafted years before in order to start running the farm for her mean old grandma.

Hell, he'd stayed even after his wife ran off and became a singer because by that time, it was his home. And for a while, he'd hoped she might find her way back home to Blackberry Cove. To him.

Now she was back. Damian sighed and dug his good boots out of the narrow closet. The day hadn't been a total waste. He'd spent more time fixing Kendall's messes and mistakes than doing any actual farm work, but he had to give her credit for sticking in there. By mid-afternoon her pink and blonde hair was covered in dried goat milk and hay and her designer jeans were torn in three very unfashionable locations. Her once sparkly boots had been covered in the same brown gunk he'd been coated with.

But she'd laughed and charmed the damn dog as well as the ornery-ass donkey that faithfully guarded the goats, but treated him like a servant. He'd fallen into her orbit again and had to remind himself what she really was: a two-timing, backstabbing, runaway wife.

He walked out of the cabin, feeling a bit ridiculous and traitorous despite repeatedly convincing himself that it was in fact Kendall who was the traitor. He stood on the porch and surveyed the property before him. He loved how he could still feel the cool breeze and taste the salt on the air though the ocean was nearly five miles away. He breathed it in, the salty air, the crisp bite to the evening, the dirt, and the animals. He'd made this place everything it was. He'd made it into a home. Mary Ellen had sat back on her ramshackle porch, the one she wouldn't let him replace, and let him take over everything but her house. She'd watched as he'd slowly turned the weedy pile of dust and rotted outbuildings into a flourishing organic vegetable and goat products farm. Never encouraging, but neither discouraging. Just watching and signing off on the various things he'd set in front of her, like the loan paperwork or the customer and vendor agreements.

Damian was self-aware enough to realize he was a cliché, the way he'd poured all his heartache and buried his anger on this farm as readily as he'd the poured concrete and dug the trenches. And he sure as hell wasn't letting Kendall take the one thing he had left, the one thing he'd made for himself despite her betrayal.

He could see across the yard between them through her window where she paced in the back of her kitchen waving her arms and talking into her cell phone dramatically. Probably talking to her agent or lawyer. Damian bit down and ground his teeth, his jaw aching. She wasn't taking a damn thing from him. And, honestly, he didn't give a shit

43

what she did or where she went once she left this time, only that she left for good. Because that would be the agreement once she signed over the other half of the property and business to him. She'd get her money, her way out, as long as she promised to never darken his door again.

He clenched his fists and walked back into his house before remembering that Kendall Kelly wasn't his problem and she hadn't been for a very, very long time. She wasn't taking anything from him again and she would only be there a few weeks.

Slamming the door shut and turning the radio up so he could finish dressing, Damian heard a familiar song blaring over his newly installed hidden speakers. A song sung by an angel with a slight razor's edge marring the nearly perfect voice, adding a punkish twinge. The music hard like ocean boulders beaten over and over by the wave of words full of pain and unfathomable loneliness.

Kendall's voice. Kendall's words. Their shattered life on the radio for the world to share their private pain. And then a lyric he didn't remember ever hearing. Actually after listening to her first album over and over he'd avoided her music as much as possible, which hadn't been difficult if he stayed on the farm and worked until he fell into bed each night. Exhausted and alone. But these quiet lines in an otherwise dark ballad caught his attention.

Where time bends, we'll meet again at the sea of broken promises
Where I gave myself to you and you called me your forever.

Had she written that about them and the first time he'd really kissed her…not the sweet soft meeting of mouths on the porch of the cottage, but a devouring innocence-stealing announcement of lust, and proclamation of impropriety? He'd never forget the day they'd hiked down the Central River and ended up at a bluff overlooking the ocean. They'd climbed down the rocks and walked for a mile or so before coming across a strange little cave with a tree growing off the side of the mouth. Kendall had insisted it was a brilliant tree that had endured the sand and the sea to thrive there on its own. She'd looked so damn beautiful with her blonde hair whipping around her face and her cheeks pink with cold.

He hadn't had a choice, he hadn't had control of his body any longer, and he'd reached out and wrapped his hand around the back of her neck and pulled her close before cradling her face in his hands. She'd smiled sweetly—the sexy-cute way her lips curved up at the edges killed him every time. And he'd kissed her hard. Not like their other soft exchanges, but with promise and possession. He belonged to her then and she to him and there had been no question otherwise.

Christ. He would never be free of her despite all his bluster and anger. She would never truly be gone from his heart, would she?

ALTHOUGH KENDALL WASN'T usually prone to fits of moping, she felt quite deserving of a good sullen pity party where she could despair about her current state of affairs and definitely not think about Damian's date. After showering and throwing on some old sweats and a sweatshirt, she called her former agent and ranted, begged for advice and then resigned herself to living in Blackberry Cove for the next few weeks. She rattled around her grandmother's ancient kitchen and fixed herself a cup of chamomile tea before stepping out onto the rotting back porch, making a quick note on her phone to run to the builder store in town the next day to price out wood for a new deck.

The broken planks groaned under her slippered feet, but that was nothing new. That old porch had complained for decades every time someone set foot on it. But two steps from the bench she'd planned to park herself on for an hour or so, she heard a loud snap followed by a quiet crunch. Her stomach dropped and then lurched to her throat as her body fell through a gaping wooden hole that opened around her foot and swallowed her leg. A sharp pain shot through her ankle like a bullet and hot tea splashed over her front as her cup fell with a thud. A scream ripped from her throat and she threw her arms wide to keep from falling completely into the hole. The pain flowed out from her foot and moved up her leg, but she was already being pulled up, strong hands gently tugging her from the now Kendall-sized crater in the porch.

"It's all right, sweetheart," Damian's deep voice soothed her. "I've got you." He tugged her onto his lap, holding her gently as his hands roamed down her body checking for wounds. She hissed as he skimmed over her right ankle. Cursing, he moved his hands up to her face and cupped her jaw, staring into her eyes. "Anywhere else?"

Even with pain radiating from her ankle and adrenaline surging through her veins, she could get lost in the green and gold depths of those eyes. How many times had she done just that as he held her close, as close as two people could be?

His fingers tightened around the back of her head. "Kendall? Are you hurt anywhere else? Did you hit your head?"

"No," she said quietly, not wanting to move, not caring about the aching throb in her ankle, or the growing thrum between her legs. Only wanting to stay there, in Damian Sloane's arms, his eyes locked on hers. But then that sharp ache moved back to her chest. And she remembered that she'd given him up a long time ago. She'd traded in his love for a more noble cause or so she'd told herself a million times since she'd walked away. "No, I'm fine. My ankle hurts a little."

He crept his fingers up into her hairline and she felt a tremor move through her body as they began to caress the back of her head. Oh God. She couldn't do this. Damian's hands on her body hurt, but it was when they were gone that the real agony took hold. She didn't pull away instead she tucked her cheek against his chest…his hard broad chest. And he let her, his hand continuing to stoke her hair.

"It's scraped up pretty bad and turning purple. You need a doctor." His chest was so warm. She luxuriated in the rumble of his voice against her cheek. He felt like he always had, like safety and warmth. Like home. She wanted to stay right there forever. Instead she pulled back a little and looked up at him.

"Oh you know me, I'm such a klutz. It's already starting to feel better." She slapped his chest lightly, going for playful but achieving only awkward. "Go on your date, Damian. If you'll just help me into the house, I'll be fine."

"Shut up, Kendall," he said and in one elegant movement he stood with her in his arms. Her hands went instinctively around his neck as he carried her into the living room where he set her on the couch and covered her with the old blue quilt folded there. Then he pulled his phone from his pocket and stepped out on to the porch. She could hear him speaking on the phone, but couldn't make out his words. Was he canceling his date? She tried not to picture the person on the other end of the call, not wanting to visualize the kind of woman Damian was attracted to now. Not wanting to burn the image of him kissing someone else, touching someone else into her brain. But, of course, he had to have been with plenty of women since her.

Damian was a gorgeous, built cowboy with freaking abs of steel and wide muscled shoulders. Even back in high school girls had clamored for his attention. She took a shuddering breath and closed her eyes.

Damian wasn't hers anymore. How many times did she need to remind herself of that?

She opened her eyes when she heard the door open and close again. "I called my mom to come check on that ankle. Let me take a look and make sure you're not hurt anywhere else." Despite the pain in her foot, Kendall scrambled to sit up, her heart pounding so hard she could hear it in her eardrums.

Kendall could carry a lot. Hell, she'd been carrying it all on her shoulders for a very long time. But all these things were starting to pile up: Ben stealing from her, her contract cancellation, her sister's and grandmother's deaths, seeing Damian again. They were a giant hastily stacked Jenga tower about ready to tumble down all around her. And the prospect of seeing Dr. Evelyn Sloane again was the straw that might just break her camel's back, that last block that throws everything into the kind of hurricane-like wreckage you just can't put back together.

"No, no, no. I'm fine," she said, wincing as pain throbbed up her leg when she finally made it into a sitting position.

Damian gently rearranged her and set a cushion under her foot. "No, you're not."

He stood next to the couch and ran his long fingers through his dark still-wet hair. A single drop of water rolled down the side of his neck and she had the sudden impulse to hop up and lick it off. She'd obviously caught him in the middle of getting ready for his date. His hair was damp and uncombed, his plaid western shirt was still unbuttoned, and the view under that shirt was magnificent. Lean, hard muscle ridged his chest and abdomen. Light hair dusted his chest and narrowed down into a light trail that disappeared into his half-buttoned jeans. Her pain-addled brain had no trouble filling in the dots of what hid beneath those button-fly jeans.

"Hey, eyes up here," he said crouching down and tipping her chin up toward his face, a smug curve of his mouth confirming she'd been caught staring quickly disappeared and was replaced with that hard grim line he wore constantly now. "I'm not exactly thrilled about seeing my mother either, but you're hurt and she's a doctor."

Damian's fingers on her chin burned, scorched like they'd been sitting in fire. He stared into her eyes with a matching heated glare, but his tone was bleak, resigned. He wasn't asking, he was telling her the way it was. But she had to wonder just what he meant by not wanting to see his mom. Despite how much his parents disapproved of her and Damian's relationship, he'd always been fairly close to Evelyn. What had happened to change all that? And if Evelyn wasn't in contact with her son any longer then his dad was probably out of the picture too. And the rift she thought she might have imagined at the attorney's office might actually be real.

So who did Damian have left? She knew from her grandma that his twin, Duncan, hadn't been home since he'd joined the Navy at eighteen. Maybe this woman he was dating was all he had? When they'd been together he'd been friends with a group of guys from his high school football team, although most had drifted away during the first two years of their marriage. Some had gone off to school, some had paired off and married young like they had, and then others moved on to other areas. Were any of them still Damian's friends?

Her heart ached more than her ankle at how little she actually knew about her husband—the one man she'd ever loved, the one man she could never have again—and the life he had now. And when the sound of tires driving up the unpaved driveway snapped his gaze away, it took his warm fingers too, leaving behind a blistering coldness. Damian stood and buttoned his shirt before turning and stalking to the door.

She wanted to thank him for helping her, ask him to hold her if only for just a minute more. But instead she called out, "I'm really okay. Nothing a warm bath and some rest won't fix. No need for you to see your mother or to miss your date…"

He stopped before walking out onto the front porch and

braced his hand on the open door frame. He dipped his head for a moment as if to gather his words and then, without turning, he growled, "Just so we're clear, sweetheart, you're no longer in charge here."

If she'd tried to predict what he was going to say at that moment she wouldn't have guessed anything close to the almost guttural snarl he'd directed at her. And, dammit, if the fiery tension that was building between them didn't feel a lot like anger now and a lot less like sex.

"Then who is?" was the not-so-clever comeback she returned.

Slowly, he turned to look at her with a surprisingly feral smile, one that made her even angrier, but also made her feel all kinds of tingly things down between her legs. That look was not one she'd ever seen on Damian's Sloane's face. It was a smile, yes, but it was also cruel and sensual and hard all at once.

"I am," he said and walked through the doorway, leaving her staring after him.

Chapter Four

D AMIAN STOOD ON the front porch and kicked at the boards, watching as his mom parked her car. Well, at least the deck seemed a little stronger than the one in back. Probably due to less direct sunlight, he thought absently, still a bit rattled from hearing Kendall scream and then holding her in his arms.

He took a deep breath.

Might as well get this over with.

His mother was standing next to her cream-colored luxury car clutching her medicine bag to her chest like a shield. It had been more a year since he'd seen her up close since he avoided both his parents as much as possible, often opting to stay on the farm and sending his employees on errands instead of going himself. The lines around her eyes seemed more prominent, but everything else was the same. Same dark hair in a clean bob, same polite smile, same tailored clothes. His mom, only perhaps a little older and carrying a little more sadness.

"Hey, Mom." He tugged at his collar, suddenly restless and a little uncomfortable.

"Hello, son." She turned to him with a watery smile as tears began to trail down her face. "Dammit. I told myself I wouldn't do this," she said wiping the dampness from her cheeks and feigning a laugh. "I'm just so glad you called."

All these tears. God, he was such a dick. The women in his life seemed to cry an awful lot lately. All he'd ever wanted was to make them happy, his mother and his wife, and yet he only seemed to bring them such grief and despair.

"Thanks for coming," Damian said flatly. He was glad she was here, but the whole situation was just so screwed up. His estranged wife had fallen through the rotting deck as he was getting ready for a date so he'd had to call his mother, whom he hadn't exchanged more than a few dozen words with since Kendall had left, despite his mother's efforts. Fucking great. As uncomplicated as a supercomputer.

"Of course," she said quietly reaching for him. He dodged her hand and turned to lead her back up the steps and into the old farmhouse. "I'm so glad you called me."

He stopped on the first step and turned back to her. Dr. Evelyn Sloane.

"Bullshit, Mom. You never liked her. Neither of you did. Kendall was never good enough for the great Sloane family."

"Your father…" So now his mom was going to blame his dad for this mess. Typical. No one ever took responsibility for their behavior anymore.

"What, Mom? What about him?" Damian knew he was raising his voice, and probably shouldn't be yelling at his mom when she should be helping Kendall, but he was so tired of all this drama. He was exhausted by the aching well of nothingness in the pit of his stomach. Goddamn Kendall for bringing it all back up to the surface again. And goddamn him for getting sucked into her vortex.

His mother grabbed his wrist and this time he let her. "I didn't know what he did."

"What are you talking about?" His dad certainly had been a dick about their relationship, so much so that he often wondered if his father had something against Kendall and her family other than being poor.

"Damian, she didn't tell you?"

A chill slid through his veins. What? Had they done something to Kendall? When? "Tell me what?" he asked, keeping his voice low.

"You don't know." Her grip on his wrist tightened and he saw lines around her eyes and mouth he'd never seen before.

"What the hell are you talking about, Mom? What did you do? What did you *do*?" The chill turned to ice and froze his chest, making it hard to breathe.

"Your dad, Damian. He had a conversation with her the night before she disappeared, but I didn't know until recently. He said something when Kendall's grandma died."

"With Kendall?"

"Yes." She held up her hand. "I don't know what they discussed. He wouldn't tell me. He just said she probably wouldn't stick around."

"Why didn't you tell me this? Why are you telling me now?"

"I didn't know until it was way too late. And I thought you knew. I thought she would have told you. You were so close. And then when she left I thought we could be there for you, but you just faded away. And then both my sons were gone. One off somewhere across the globe and the other one only miles away but still just as inaccessible," his mother said, her voice cracking, sounding frail and old for the first time.

"Kendall never said anything. Other than a bullshit note about not being in love with me and needing to make it on her own. I don't really know why she left. I just...I just thought...I don't know. I thought that she had been biding her time until she could go pursue her music." But had he really believed that? Or had there always been an unsettled niggling in the back of his mind that there had been something else that had chased her away?

"She loved you, Damian. I think she left because she loved you. I think..."

"Stop. I...please just stop." He yanked his hand away and ran it over his face. Kendall was in pain and this was not the time to go unraveling the mystery of his wayward wife.

"Damian. Honey. I believe he drove her away. And that she left because he somehow convinced her that it would be better for you if she did."

"I can't do this right now," he said a little too forcibly, he realized when his mom flinched. "We can talk about it later."

"When, Damian? We've wasted so much time." Her eyes were wide, pleading.

"Later. I promise. But not now. She's hurt and let's just focus on that for now."

"I need you back in my life, son. I miss my children," she cried and he heard the sadness and felt the years of pain in her voice. And, for once, he realized that he might not be the only one who had suffered through the several years. He heard so much regret; she was so desperate to make it right that Damian softened and patted her hand.

"Later, Mom. Later. Not that it matters now anyway," he mumbled. The past was the past. And just because Kendall was in town for a couple weeks didn't change anything.

She nodded and he led her up the steps and into the old farmhouse where Kendall lay curled into a ball with her head on the arm of the couch. Her eyes were closed but her fingers tapped on her wrist. She was awake and she was clearly agitated, but fighting it. Kendall Kelly was beautiful even now after she'd hurt him so mercilessly, even now that she so casually insisted he go on his date with another woman. Even now after she wafted her perfect little ass back into town to stir up a bunch of dead and buried ashes.

"Kendall, you remember my mom." Kendall's eyes snapped open and it was hard to miss the tightness of her jaw as her finger stopped tapping and she pushed herself to a sitting position. He lunged forward to help her, and didn't miss her wince when she pushed upright.

"Dr. Sloane." Kendall held herself rigid and gave his mom an awkward smile. "You didn't have to come."

"Hello, Kendall. Oh, honey, don't jostle around." His mother crouched down near the end of the couch and nodded at Kendall for permission to lift the blanket. "I know I'm probably the last person you wanted to see today, but let's take a look at that ankle, shall we?" His mom lifted the blanket and tenderly felt around Kendall's swelling ankle. "It looks like a sprain. I'd like to get it x-rayed just to make sure you don't have a hairline fracture."

Damian stood next to the couch, resisting the urge to reach down and hold Kendall's hand, pushing down his instinct to comfort her. Strange that after so many seething, bitter years his desire to protect her overrode his need to make her suffer, to punish her for turning him into the shell of a man he was now. But her confident, almost sanguine, stare at his mom and the way she swallowed down her discomfort reminded him of the old Kendall. The Kendall he'd known before. The one he'd fallen madly in love with was so strong, an oak in a family full of wilted lettuce. Not the cowardly girl who had run away from him, or the brazenly phony woman he'd seen on TV. This was who he'd always thought she was. But was she really? What kind of woman left without any word? One day they'd been married and so in love they shared everything and the next day she was gone.

He choked down the anger surging up. It could wait. Making her pay for her betrayal could wait until he knew she would be okay. And, yes, he fully realized what a hypocritical asshole he was.

His mother tenderly wrapped Kendall's ankle and wrote something on her prescription pad and handed it to him. "Can you bring her by the hospital after you pick up this prescription for pain?" She looked down at Kendall with an odd look on her face. A look that seemed a lot like sympathy, almost motherly. A look that made his chest ache so hard he yanked the small note from his mother's hand before he got lost in it.

All this warm-and-fuzzy-feelings shit was starting to get on his nerves. Yeah, great his mom was finally being kind to his wife…his soon-to-be *ex*-wife. So what. Too little too late.

"Sure," he said and shoved the note in his pocket. What was he supposed to do? What did they expect from him? Forgiveness? Love? Forget it. Too much water under that bridge. "Thanks for coming by."

His mother stood and brushed her hands down her tailored pants. "Thank you for calling me. I'll meet you at the hospital. I'm sure we can get her in for a quick scan." She swallowed before looking up at him again. "Damian, we really do need to talk about this."

Kendall's head jerked up to meet his gaze before looking between him and his mother and back at him again. "About what?"

Evelyn Sloane leaned down and gently smoothed down Kendall's hair, so sweetly it reminded him of when he and Duncan had been young. That ache in his chest cracked and he could feel the fissures of it running along that hard shell he'd so carefully built up over the last four years.

"About everything, Kendall. The past *and* the present."

Damian held up his hand as if that would somehow get his mother to stop talking. As if he somehow could stop any of the women in his life from doing anything. "Mom, we're not doing this now. Kendall's hurt and exhausted. We'll meet you at the hospital in an hour."

His mother's shoulders slumped slightly. Now that he'd called her she was going to see this as an opportunity to fix what was broken in their family. Problem was, there wasn't any way to fix it.

Kendall took a deep breath and did her best to smile. "Thank you for your help, Dr. Sloane. Really. But there's nothing to talk about."

Damian's mom took Kendall's small hand in hers and patted it. "Evelyn. Please call me Evelyn. And there is so much to talk about. But we'll leave it until later."

Again, Damian reminded himself that all these feelings were bullshit. He was looking for closure, sure, but another kind altogether. The kind that ended in divorce and never having to see Kendall again. Not the kind with fixed relationships and mended fences. Fairy tales weren't his thing anymore.

It was time for these tattered fences to be torn down and replaced completely.

AFTER AN HOUR of driving and waiting and more time getting an X-ray that concluded Kendall did not have anything other than some superficial scrapes and a slight sprain, Kendall found herself on familiar ground—arguing with her husband.

"No, Damian. Absolutely not." The ball in her chest that had made itself comfortable since she stepped back in town grew, stealing her breath, leaving her unsettled.

There was absolutely no way—no freaking way— Kendall was sleeping in Damian's cottage when she had a perfectly decent house just across the yard. Plus, she didn't need him babysitting her. Plus *plus*, she didn't want him that close, messing with her resolve, and her hormones. She'd been back in Blackberry Cove all of one full day and she'd attended a funeral, been tortured against her grandmother's hall wall by her not-quite-ex-husband, shoveled goat poop, showered in goat milk—which had left hair super soft, but that wasn't the point—and nearly broken her damn ankle. It was late and she was too exhausted to deal with anyone or anything. Especially one very hot and very bossy cowboy who had refused to leave her side at the hospital and was now carting her from his truck into the cottage.

As he pushed open the door and carried her into the re-furbished cabin she sucked in a breath and closed her eyes.

This isn't happening. This isn't happening. Dammit, this is happening.

Kendall's heart tilted sideways and threatened to jump from her chest. Leaning her head against Damian's rock-like chest, she burrowed further into his arms. She didn't want to be there, in the place that used to be their home together. She didn't want to see how it had changed, how it was no longer hers and how perhaps other women—he had to have had girlfriends over the years—had made their imprint on what was supposed to have been her life, her love, her home.

"Kendall, open your eyes."

She squeezed them tighter, wanting to keep it all out, everything—her mother leaving her, Nana's and Sabre's deaths, running away from life, broken promises. All of it. Though her grandmother had never shown her traditional love she had given her a home. The only real one she'd ever known. And she was feeling wrapped in a thick blanket of sadness as she mourned the cranky old woman. As she mourned the sister she barely knew. As she mourned the life she'd never have—not the music business, but the business of the farm and being a farmer's wife. And she knew the second she opened her eyes it would all come rushing at her double speed, a rubber band full of memories snapping back and hitting her straight in the chest. And she wouldn't be able to keep in the tears she'd been holding on to. Not the silly little waterfall she'd let go the night before. No, those tears had been a mere pressure release. The real ones were just waiting for her control to slip…because once she let them go she didn't know if she'd ever be able to stop.

"Kendall," he commanded and she snuggled in more, crushing her face to his warm body. She knew she had no right to cling to him. Of course not. She'd abdicated that throne long ago. But she was selfish and she wanted to curl into him for just another moment until she was forced back into the real world again. The shitty world she was solely responsible for creating for herself.

"It's just a house, Kendall," Damian said flatly.

Taking a deep breath she nodded against him, letting the soft flannel of his shirt caress her cheek. When his breath mirrored hers with a sigh, slowly she lifted her head and opened her eyes.

It wasn't exactly what she had expected, or what she'd been so afraid of, but their cute little rustic cabin looked just like an updated cute, but much bigger and more modern rustic cabin. The kitchen, which opened into a beamed great room, was all new and sparkling, but still had that country vintage feel. It was all the same but very much different. Like they'd planned together so many years ago.

Patiently Damian held her, not saying anything, only turning slowly as she took everything in. The black and white marble counter and the small, but sturdy wood block island, the retro-styled refrigerator and stove in mint the only splashes of color in the diminutive, but well-appointed kitchen. A small counter divided the open living area from the kitchen. The oversized sectional couch was warm dark brown leather with a few throw pillows in mint and beige. A large barn door coffee table dominated the room, but gave it a comfortable feel. The old dusty cabin was now a lived-in and lovely home.

Damian's home.

"It's beautiful," she said quietly as he set her on the couch and pulled a large blanket over her. Before he pulled away she gripped his flannel shirt and held him close. "Your..." She stumbled over that first word and swallowed hard. "Your home is beautiful, Damian." Her words were colored by their past. Tainted by their present. And dark with knowing that they had no future together. The ball in her chest grew bigger, making it harder to breathe, making it harder to think.

For the first time since she'd been back to town, which seemed like weeks instead of hours, he looked down at her with something a little less than resentment and a little more like compassion. For one single tiny second she wanted to grab on to that look and bury herself there forever. Never run, never leave, never move on. Maybe it was the fall that was making her weak, maybe it was the medication Evelyn had given her. Either way she felt herself letting go of the rigid hold on her resolve and felt herself leaning in to the tiny sliver of hope she glimpsed in Damian's eyes.

His large hand smoothed down her side and though her clothes and the blanket separated her skin from his and the pills had numbed her senses, she responded as if he caressed her directly, sucking in a sharp breath and letting her eyes drift shut.

"We'll talk later, sweetheart. Sleep now." Kendall wanted to talk now. She wanted to tell him the truth. The reasons why she'd left. He'd understand now, wouldn't he? And maybe he would tell her it was okay and that they could live in this little cottage for the rest of their lives. Like they'd always planned.

She drifted off to the soft sounds of her husband moving around in the kitchen and a quiet memory of them riding horses together down on the beach.

Chapter Five

AFTER SEEING TO the animals, Damian started a fire in the wood-burning stove and poured himself a much taller than was appropriate glass of whiskey before settling himself into the chair across from his couch. The couch where his runaway wife—perhaps soon-to-be ex-wife—lay sleeping.

A long pale pink strand of hair had tugged loose from her ponytail, falling across her cheek where a soft huff of breath occasionally lifted it from her face. He was mesmerized by that little length of her hair. In a strange way almost jealous of it. But instead of reaching across the table and tucking the cotton-candy-colored strand back behind her ear—because, let's face it, he couldn't really handle touching her again—he picked up his glass and swirled the amber liquid before drinking it down in one very aggressive gulp. He savored the bright burn down his throat and the immediate softening of *fucking feelings.*

Kendall mumbled in her sleep and rolled onto her back, kicking the blanket off and throwing her leg over the back of the couch.

Goddamn her. For coming back. For leaving in the first place. For getting hurt. For hurting him. But mostly for getting back under his skin and cracking his chest wide open. Without. Even. Trying.

When he'd called Carissa to postpone their date he could hear the disappointment in her voice, followed shortly thereafter by censure when he explained his reason for bailing. Clearly he had no right to be offended. Hell, he was technically a married man—he had no place dating anyone until he finally signed the divorce papers.

Automatically his eyes flicked to his desk sitting in the shadows against the far wall.

Damian checked his watch; it was after midnight. He should get his tired ass up out of this chair and get Kendall into his bed. Well, not that way. Okay, maybe that way.

Shit.

What did he want?

If he sat here staring at her like some weirdo creeper he certainly wasn't acting like a pissed-off ex who couldn't wait to get his pain-in-the-ass wife out of his hair for good. Nope. If he was being honest with himself, and it was more than time for that, he was still acting like that pathetic bastard who mooned over her for years while he had her and then more after she left.

"Damian…" Kendall's voice was slurred from sleep and the sound was sweet with history.

"Yeah, baby?" The endearment came out automatically,

just like the sweethearts he kept trying to unsuccessfully make sound condescending.

She turned to her side and propped her cheek on her palm. "What are you still doing up?"

"I had to make sure the animals were fed and locked up. Still need to keep an eye on the two pregnant does that seem ready to pop any minute. I also grabbed your clothes and put them in the bedroom." He flicked his gaze toward the bedroom door. "I was getting ready to take you back there. I'll settle in on the couch." He stood and moved toward her at the same time she swung her legs to the floor and stood up.

"Dammit, Kendall." He lunged forward when she wobbled. His hands found her shoulders dramatically though she didn't seem to need much help. "Why won't you let me help you?"

"I know you don't want to." She looked up defiantly. "I know you don't want anything to do with me."

"Don't pretend you know what I want. You don't know anything about me."

"Don't growl at me, Damian Sloane. I'm trying to have a conversation with you. For once."

"Look, sweetheart, you don't set the rules anymore. The days of me following you around like a lovelorn puppy are over."

"So basically you're asserting your right to growl at me? You must feel so empowered." She glared up at him and then slowly, deliberately rolled her eyes and sighed emphatically. "I'm fine. I can walk. In fact, a couple over-the-counter pain meds and I'll be good to go."

She tugged from his grasp and the heat in his veins burned. "Quit walking away from me," he said, his voice perhaps a little louder than he'd intended, but it stopped her retreat. His words hung in the air between them so heavy and full of unspoken meaning. That was the crux of it all, wasn't it? How easy it was to literally and figuratively walk away from him. He was an idiot. An idiot making a big deal about nothing.

Slowly she turned, steady on her feet, and set her hands on her hips. "I'm just getting some water."

He took a step toward her. "I can get you some water, Kendall."

The corner of her mouth tipped up slightly. "Are you going to pee for me too, cowboy? Because that's next up on the agenda."

"Don't be ridiculous."

"Hey, just giving you a heads-up." She didn't smile, but she did take the water and the two pills he handed her. She swallowed them down and set the glass back on the counter, then rubbed her hand over the marble.

She looked around the open room, her gaze landing on the built-in cabinets that took up the whole far wall of the cottage, and he suddenly felt heavy, frozen. Slowly she moved toward the wall, her hand almost mindlessly trailing

69

along the counter, the old stuffed chair he'd bought on consignment in Davis two years before, and then the couch he'd bought new from an online supplier. It wasn't exactly like the one they'd picked out together, but he suddenly realized how very close it actually was.

Standing in front of the rough-hewn shelves with her long striped ponytail a mess down her back, the angry pulse of Damian's heart slowed and he was filled with a hollow longing, the very same one that plagued him the first couple years after she left. A deep echoing well of want and need— and instead of the answering rage that used to quell it, he felt only an aching sadness for him and this beautiful broken woman.

Without realizing it he had taken the few steps across the room to reach her side. For a long, swollen moment as her eyes skimmed the books he thought she might miss it, and he wasn't quite sure if he was relieved or disappointed. But then she slowly raised her finger and pushed aside the fallen copy of a goat-breeding book and pressed into the unpainted wood at the back of the built-in.

She made a small sound, like a soft gasp or little sigh, and he turned to stare at her profile. So much beauty in such a feisty little package. She had been everything he'd ever wanted. But she had run from him, from their life here in Blackberry Cove.

She's here now.

Though she'll be gone again soon enough.

But maybe she wasn't meant to be here. Maybe she really did have bigger and better things to do out in the world. Things that didn't include a goat farmer and a family history of abandonment and disdainful neglect. Maybe he could love her while she was here and then let her go, give her back to the world when she was ready to leave.

Damian's temples burned and the back of his throat felt lined in sandpaper. The thought of not holding on to his resentment and bitterness and actually giving her what she needed felt uncomfortable but right.

He looked back at her finger as it traced the carved heart in the wood and the roughly etched D and K just barely illuminated in the low light of the fire and the single lit lamp. He had never meant for her to see the old tree carving. Well, he had at one time. He'd had the idea in his head for a year or so before they were married. He'd planned to incorporate it into the redesign of the cottage. One day.

But then she turned to him and the look in her eyes was soft and haunted. He could take her anger—he knew what to do with that. Hell he just used it as fuel for his own rage and bitterness. Easy fucking peasy.

The darkness in those normally crystal blue eyes didn't belong just to him. It was built and crafted over years, years of trying to get love from a family that didn't know how to love. And then flip-flopping and acting like she didn't give a shit about anything until him. And then stomping all over that. But for the first time he saw more.

This time he saw regret. So much that it made it hard to hold her gaze, made it harder to stay pissed. But he didn't want to soften his jagged edges. He didn't want her to soothe or smooth any of the bitterness he'd need for when she left again. Because this connection, this zing of energy when he touched her skin or was within a dozen feet of her wasn't real. Not for her. And his salty anger was the only thing that kept him moving forward.

But that single tear that welled in her eye and stayed suspended for what seemed like hours finally became too swollen and ran down her cheek. God, she was so heartbreakingly beautiful.

And so not mine anymore.

Damian wanted to kiss that fucking tear away and then lift her into his arms and screw the darkness out of her, out of himself. He reached out and cupped her delicate jaw in his hand, wiping away the wetness with his thumb. But before he could kiss her or lift her into his arms, she gave him a soft smile and wrapped her cool hand around his wrist.

"I'm so very sorry," she whispered. "For everything." Her eyes never left his.

"You *were* my life, Kendall." Horrified at the shake in his voice, he dropped his hand and took a step back. He wouldn't let her drag him down this road. The road where she told him her ridiculous reason for fucking up their lives—well his life anyway since hers seemed to have taken off like a rocket ship—and he was supposed to forgive her.

Then they'd bang and she'd go back to her glam rock star life and he'd go back to his pathetic excuse for a life.

"I never wanted to hurt you. I only…" She closed her eyes and took a deep breath. "I thought I was giving you back your life."

"Bullshit." He practically spat the word. But her eyes didn't squint in signal of an oncoming rage, they just looked more sunken. Shadowed. "You did what you did because you're selfish. And a coward."

She took a step closer to him, erasing the space he'd put between them. Her hands were clenched at her sides and her lips parted as if she might disagree with him, but then she closed them again. She nodded. "Yes. I am. I'm all that and more."

Dammit. She was tearing him apart all over again with those sad eyes.

"What do you want from me, Kendall? I told you I'd buy you out. And I will. I'll take care of you while you're here. But I can't give you anything else. I can't give you what I don't have."

She nodded and moved toward the kitchen without a limp. Her foot was obviously already healing. "I would take whatever you had to give." And against his will and his better judgment he felt his blood turn hot and his traitorous dick go half hard. This woman and her words. Even after everything she'd put him through, her unintended double meaning could flip his switch from off to on in an instant.

73

"I can only give you tonight," he said not fully meaning it. Knowing that one night with his wife would never be enough, but it was all they would get. Slowly he held his hand out, palm up.

IF KENDALL WAS honest with herself, honesty being a relatively new concept she was still getting fully acquainted with, she would have to admit that she never expected Damian to reach for her with anything other than irritation in his eyes. No, she might have dreamed it over and over and in vivid detail just about every night since she left him, but she'd never thought he would.

But there he was, the one man she'd ever loved, holding out his hand to her, giving her the choice to put her hand in his. And it wasn't anything close to love in his eyes, but it wasn't irritation. And it was the promise of lying under him for one night, showing him with her body that she'd never loved another and never would.

That thick band tightened around her chest when she realized what it was.

Lust.

Damian wanted her. Maybe not in the same way she wanted him, but hell if she wasn't going to take another opportunity to be in his arms again. She'd deal with the fallout of it all tomorrow…and probably every day after that.

Tonight, she would show him with her body what she had never been brave enough to tell him. That despite his pure love for her, she'd been a coward at the root of it all. And just like a cavity, that rot had spread and infected the whole of her. She knew it would have been a matter of time before it destroyed him too. And he had been the one good thing she'd ever had or done.

There was no way she would ruin that.

No. Way.

She closed her eyes briefly and took a deep breath. Maybe tonight she could love him enough for the both of them. She would have no expectations and not be afraid to give him everything…and then walk away. But maybe this time it would be with her head held high and not scurrying off in the middle of the night with her tail between her legs.

Taking a step closer she put her hand in his palm and watched as his rough work-worn fingers closed around it.

"I don't expect—"

"Stop." He put his fingers over her mouth and they weren't just warm, they were on fire, fire that shot directly from her mouth to her core and between her legs. And that tight band squeezed tighter and tighter until it snapped. Before she could think about what she was doing she pressed her body up against Damian's and wrapped her free hand around his neck. She took a second to breathe him in, the natural scent of a man mixed with the comfort of the land he worked like it was his religion, and to appreciate his long, tall body and how hers just fit with his despite their significant height difference. She'd always felt like she was vertically challenged until she was in Damian's arms where she fit perfectly, the nut to his screw.

When his hands reached down and curved around her butt she took a deep breath. She was going all in. He leaned down and her eyes fluttered shut—it was too much. He was too much and the air was too thick with the tension between them and the murky fog of their history. When his lips touched hers, they were soft, full. He didn't devour her like he had before. Well he did, but much, much slower.

The butterflies in her belly liquefied and slowly slid down into the V between her legs. When his mouth finally touched hers it was firm and soft but less insistent, less forceful than their kisses before. Her hand shook as they moved from the back of his neck around to the front of his face, his scruffy sweet face. He kissed her so painfully sweetly that it almost hurt. No, it did hurt but in that decadent, lazy, deep way that also felt so addictively good.

Damian's fingers gripped harder on her flannel-covered bottom, biting into her skin. She hoped he'd leave marks, evidence of his touch that she could look at in the mirror and run her fingers over, remembering her last time with her husband. As he lifted her up, her legs automatically encircled his waist. Just like they always did. Muscle memory was a bitch.

No. She wasn't going there. Not this time. Kendall knew

what this was all about. This was her last chance, her final shot at love—no not love, that was done and this thing between them was always going to be one-sided. This was lust. This was an opportunity to say goodbye for real. For good.

With the strength that had always astonished her, impressed her, made her feel so safe, he continued to kiss her as he walked her back toward the couch. She tried to ignore the pinch of disappointment that pooled in her chest when she realized he wasn't taking her to his bed.

But, she reminded herself, she would take what he was willing to give. She would take it and stuff it away and bring it back out when inevitably the road got rough and the loneliness got too bleak.

When he turned them and sat on the couch with her straddling his lap, Damian moved his hands to her hips and pulled back. When he didn't say anything Kendall opened her eyes to find him staring at her. She knew he found her lacking, that he could see all the ugliness that was covered by her pink hair and contrived exterior. He knew what she was. He always had.

A fraud. A fake from the most broken of dysfunctional families. He was probably thinking what a big mistake he'd made offering her his hand. Damian was no fool. He was better than her and always had been.

"Are you sure you're not in pain?" he asked. Her surprise must have shown on her face because the corner of his mouth turned up with just a hint of a smile. "What? You thought I was going to turn down a hot woman in my lap?"

"Well you *were* on your way to a date earlier." She shrugged.

"Kendall, we're not talking about anything except this right here." He squeezed her hips and gave her a pointed look. "But we will talk. Later."

What was left to talk about? He would have never understood why she left four years ago, any more than he would now. What did it matter anyway? What's done was done. Nothing good ever came from the truth. Only heartache and disappointment.

But she wanted this night with him. She suspected it might actually hinge on her agreement to discuss the past. And didn't Damian deserve some answers, some closure? A path to take. Her heart stuttered at the thought of him of moving on. With someone else.

Tamping down her fear, Kendall simply nodded. She could give him that. Hell, it's the least she could give him.

Damian's answering grin was so far from happy and so close to predatory that Kendall wondered if she'd survive one more night with her husband, with the man she thought of as her soul mate. If he'd end up blasting apart the few remaining chunks of her dilapidated shields.

But then he kissed her again and she was lost in the slick slide of his tongue against hers.

Chapter Six

D AMIAN HAD BEEN seconds away from choking on all the ridiculous and flowery words that threatened to spill from his mouth so he shut himself up by kissing Kendall. And damn if it didn't feel like coming home every damn time he touched her, and even more so when he kissed her. The matching glide of their tongues somehow made him less broken, less jagged when she was near.

Which didn't make any sense since she was the one responsible for the fucked-up mess he'd become. And yet she seemed to be the only thing that assuaged the dank loneliness that plagued him. Despite their painful past, Kendall was everything bright and beautiful in the world. She had been the light that kept his inherent darkness from overpowering him. And when she'd left him she'd taken that light with her.

Growing up, his brother and he had been their own normalcy. And while Duncan had always been more the rebel, getting in trouble constantly, Damian had been the rule follower, but not always with resentment. He'd never wanted to be a lawyer, never wanted anything other than to work the land. When Duncan joined the Army, Damian had been forced to deal with his future on his own. He'd decided even before he'd seen Kendall that day that he was not going away to college. But then she was there and his decision to stay in Blackberry Cove was final. Hell, had it even been a choice once he'd fallen for her? Probably not.

But even the strange sadness that seemed to have attached itself to her since returning to town couldn't mask the brave jut of her chin or the courage gleaming in her eyes. In a way he hated her for her strength. But he also admired it about her. His woman never gave up.

Correction. This woman was not his woman.

Regardless, the woman writhing in his arms and grinding against the erection straining against his now much tighter jeans was the epitome of courage. She was infuriatingly stubborn, cruel even, for walking away from him, from them. But she had braved her childhood like a warrior and even her current and far more public crisis.

She'd also made him suffer so perhaps he should stop focusing on how amazing, how right, she felt in his arms and start concentrating on making her see just how wrong she was for walking away. But even as he was saying it, his promise of nothing more than this night sounded hollow to him. Once he'd tasted her he wouldn't be able to not touch her while she was staying here. So at the very least this thing would continue. But beyond that, what did he want? Tomorrow. He would work that out tomorrow.

He dropped his hands and leaned back into the couch. "Take your shirt off," he demanded quietly. When she narrowed her eyes and scrunched her brows together, he ran his thumb down the center to smooth it. "Take your shirt off, Kendall."

She hesitated. Maybe because she didn't recognize this version of him, maybe because he frightened her, maybe because she didn't want to take this insane chemistry between them any further. Either way, it didn't matter. She either would or she wouldn't. But if they were doing this, then they were playing by his rules. Period.

Kendall seemed to understand that because she tugged off her T-shirt and smirked when his eyes locked on to her breasts. "No bra, huh?" He spread his hands over her hips and slowly ran them up her sides, tracing every curve, every rib, stopping with his thumbs a hair's width below the full roundness of the bottoms of her tits.

On a gasp, she said, "Changed into my pajamas. Would have made a different choice in wardrobe if I'd known."

His thumbs brushed the undersides of her breasts and his fingers cupped them, squeezing gently before dipping his head down to taste one tight bud then the other. On a shuddering moan, Kendall's head fell back, her hands flying up to grip his wrists. His answering groan was louder, deeper and full of male pride.

"Finally," he breathed out against her breast and watched as her nipple hardened and grew tighter. He luxuriated in her perfectly round breast, pinching and nipping and licking until she wriggled on his lap and her hips rubbed her center against his. He continued until she was mindless, a beautiful angel writhing and crying on his lap for release. His original plan had been to take her here on the couch, to stay out of the bedroom, which felt too intimate, too much like what might have been but wasn't and never would be. But he couldn't quite remember why he'd made that rule, or why he'd want her anywhere but in his bed.

Standing with her in his arms he walked them to the bedroom and placed her on his bed. Spread out on his bed, her pale hair was breaking free from its tie and partially spread around her head. And the way she looked at him…well, it almost hurt like a kick to his ribs. But he ignored it, ignored everything swirling around in his head because she was perfect. Stunning. And his.

Except they were both still wearing most of their clothes. He rectified that situation, tugging off her sweats and quickly removing his boots, then his shirt and pants, and threw them all somewhere behind him. Pulling the box of condoms he'd bought on impulse the day before when he'd heard Kendall was coming back to town, he thanked the universe for an idea he'd originally scoffed at. And then it was just them. Naked.

Damian had dreamed of Kendall's body nearly every night for the last four years and now that she was there he wanted to go slow, taste every inch with his tongue and touch all of the places that he knew drove her wild. But the desperation in her eyes matched the feeling thrumming through his body. And he thought he might actually die if he didn't get inside her soon.

Quickly he rolled on the condom before he placed his hands on her thighs and slowly pushed her legs wider, her body opening to him. He wanted to be in her, needed her body around his, but he also couldn't pass up the opportunity for a taste of her.

"Damian, please," she said. "Please…" The plea turned to a keening cry as he put his mouth on her and a bolt of recognition swept through him.

This. Her. It was so much, almost everything. The familiar sweet, tangy taste of her flooded his senses, filled him with something a lot like wholeness. But that was ridiculous. This was sex. Great sex. But just sex.

He dragged his tongue through her folds and felt her body quiver under his hands. When she lifted her hips and ground herself into his face, he bit down on that hard bundle of nerves and watched her face as her body arched off the bed and she fell apart.

Moving up her body, he stroked everywhere until she finally opened her eyes and looked up with the sexiest little half smile he'd ever seen and he knew time was up for both of them.

Hitching one of her legs over his shoulder and pressing the other down to the mattress he entered her in one slick thrust and settled his pelvis against hers. And stopped. To catch his breath, which sounded ragged and loud in the quiet room. To admire the beauty of the woman beneath him. To feel her lush body wrapped around his.

When she reached her hands up and cupped his face ever so gently the fire inside him exploded and every part of his body snapped and sparked until she began to move beneath him. He met her push against his body with a series of lazy thrusts in and out, all the time marveling at how perfectly their bodies matched, how their lovemaking was almost like a dance.

Damian dropped his hands and her legs wrapped around his thighs, gripping hard, clinging to him as he took over and his moves became more frantic, more erratic, deeper, hotter. Kendall's nails dug into his shoulder, and her whole body arched and she tensed. Then she sobbed his name and that was it. He was gone, dropping his head to her neck and biting down on the tendon there he was caught up in the exquisite torture of her throbbing body pulsing around his.

The realization that he had been lying on Kendall panting for God knows how long hit him. He started to roll off her, and her arms gripped him tighter around his shoulders.

"Stay. Please. Just for a minute." So he settled back between her thighs and kissed her shoulder and stroked her damp hair.

Eventually he got up to deal with the condom and the rest of newly opened box and tossed them on his side table.

"Optimistic, aren't you?" Kendall laughed, the gray sheet already covering her perfect body.

"I don't know—am I?" he asked and flipped her on her front before starting in all over again.

HOURS LATER KENDALL knew she couldn't put off the conversation she'd been avoiding for the last four years. Damian was demanding an explanation. More importantly, he deserved one. She was too soft, too raw, to be anything but honest with him at this point. Apparently he'd sexed the truth out of her with his stupid penis. His stupid magic penis.

"Later is now, sweetheart. Time to talk," Damian prompted.

"It seemed so clear-cut four years ago," she started. Because it had.

He rolled to his side, facing her, and gently ran his hand over her hip and thigh. "And now?"

She shook her head and her eyes filled with tears. The back of her throat itched. But she had to hold it together because he'd likely view her crying as bullshit crocodile tears.

"You left. I stayed. It doesn't get much simpler than that. The question is why, Kendall. Why did you leave? And why was it so easy?"

"I didn't want to." That old sick thing in her stomach

twisted like it did whenever she thought of that day, which was often. "You know it wasn't easy. You have to know that."

"Bullshit. Did you even love me at all?"

The sob she'd been pushing down broke free and she sat up, covering her mouth. She was a coward. Too afraid to face him. Too scared of everything. This was so damn hard.

"Lie back down." Damian pushed on her shoulder, his hand firm, but gentle.

She settled back on the bed but turned her head toward the wall. "I can't look at your face…"

"Tough shit, sweetheart. You owe me an explanation and I want to see your face when you tell me." This was the new Damian, the one she didn't know, the one who didn't stare at her like the sun set and rose by her command. He set his mouth in a grim line and his eyes were devoid of any affection.

Kendall sighed and turned toward him. He was right, of course, which didn't make her less annoyed or uncomfortable or afraid. Because what if the truth was as flimsy an excuse as he seemed to believe it was? What then? Had everything she'd done been for nothing? A complete waste of two lives?

She'd avoided this very moment for so long. But he was right. He was always right. Maybe that was part of the problem. Maybe that's why she thought it was okay to leave without any word other than her stupid note. Regardless, here they were and it was time to come clean.

"I left because I had to," she said swallowing past her discomfort, past the huge lump of sand in her throat. "I know you're not going to believe me. And you probably shouldn't. Never really gave you reason to trust in me. But…"

She glanced down, took another deep breath, and looked back up into his beautiful eyes—those eyes that had once viewed her with love and trust and hope now only stared back blankly.

He didn't say anything and the look on his face didn't change. He just waited. Goddamn Damian and his endless patience. He wasn't going to make this easy for her. But of course why should he? He had no reason to. He had suffered, and as far as he knew he was the only one doing all of the suffering. Damian had no idea about the endless empty ache she felt on waking every day and that grew even worse at night without him in her life.

More than anything, Kendall wanted to reach out and rub her hands over his messy dark hair, drop to her knees and soothe the pain in his heart, and save him from this, from her. But she'd tried that—that's why she'd run away. To save him, or so she told herself. "Do you remember that day? The day I left?"

A shadow crossed his face and quickly ghosted away before he simply nodded. Of course he did. "You were out in the fields fixing fences. I'd stayed home to can the blackberries and make pies for the town picnic and dance." In truth, that day was never very far away from her thoughts. But she'd gotten pretty good at pushing down all that raw jangly emotion that had scratched at her for so long. It all boiled up to the top now…and it hurt just like it was yesterday.

"Your dad came by to talk to you, but he ended up having plenty to say to me. Some hard truths that I didn't really want to hear." Damian's eyes never left her face and his expression never changed, but his hands fisted at his sides and his Adam's apple bobbed as if trying to jump out of his throat, as if he had something to say, but she needed to get the whole story out before she lost her nerve. Or worse, started crying.

"What he said was hard to hear. And it hurt… It hurt a lot. He was right though." She closed her eyes for a moment remembering that day, remembering the hope she'd felt that this was the day the Sloane family would take her into the fold. That they'd finally see her value, and how much she loved their son, and how she planned to take care of him for the rest of their lives.

"Kendall, I'm not sure there's anything he could have said that would be so bad you would leave me without telling me." Damian's voice was deep and gravelly, clearly filled with emotion that he wasn't showing but felt. He was right. He was always right.

"He told me that marrying me ruined your life. And when I chuckled and said everyone said that—that you loved me and our love would show everyone how wrong they were—he laughed. He said that you applied for the vet program at Davis and that you had been accepted."

She watched Damian's face for a response, waited for him to deny it or even confirm it. Something. She'd never truly known if Mr. Sloane had been lying or if Damian had applied for school without telling her. But she couldn't read him anymore. Other than lust or anger, the man in her bed was a virtual stranger to her. That thought made her even sadder than anything else. "He backed that up with a lot of stuff about how useless I was, how a wife like me would only hinder your chances of success, how we were only playing house. You know, the usual."

Damian rolled back on the bed and bent his arm under his head. The sheet shifted, dropping down below his waist, exposing his chiseled chest and abs, sending a flush of unexpected heat through her body at the most inappropriate time possible. Go figure: that was Kendall Kelly right there in a nutshell. Sharing her darkest of dark moments with her soon-to-be ex-husband and ogling the divots and bumps of muscle on his stomach. Again, she wanted to reach out and run her hand through his hair, tangle her fingers in the dusting of hair on his chest, drag her mouth over his tight abdominal muscles. Just to reassure herself that he was actually there with her. She shouldn't; he wouldn't want her to, not right then. But she had to. So she did.

At first she just settled her hand on his chest but she couldn't stop there. She'd always been impulsive, and when it came to him she had absolutely no control. Stroking her hand gently across his chest, she felt the muscles ripple under her hand, but he didn't pull away. Instead she kissed his hard stomach and sat back again. "I'm not sure your dad's visit alone could have chased me off. No, scratch that, no one chased me off. I left on my own. I take responsibility for that."

Damian growled under her hand causing her to stop mindlessly caressing his chest. "Then why, Kendall?" he asked almost pleadingly. The anger was still there, down beneath the betrayal, but mostly he just sounded…sad. "If it wasn't him then what? Who? You knew I loved you. Why couldn't you just trust me?"

Tears began to threaten at the backs of her eyes. Dammit, if she started crying she would never be able to finish. He really did deserve to know. He deserved closure. So that he could move on, and she could go do whatever she was going to do.

"Nana came to see me, I swear not two minutes after your dad left. God that woman was mean. It's almost like she knew I was vulnerable and she had to get there before you came home and reassured me that everything would be all right. She told me she knew why your dad was there and that she had some information that would help me make a good decision about what to do with my life. They were tag team wrestlers and their opponent was me." That was the part Kendall never really understood. Why had her grandma taken her in, when clearly she wanted nothing to do with her? Nana resented every single thing about Kendall: the way she looked, the way she talked, that she ate her food, and that she required clothes to go to school, that she was her mother's daughter. Everything.

How many nights had she cried in Damian's arms, wondering why her grandma couldn't love her? So many...too many to count. "Nana told me I had ruined your life... Surprise! Which of course she'd said a million times before. But this time she added the truth about my mother." She had repeated this story to herself for so many years that it had sort of become her little martyr mantra. She'd started to believe her own narrative that leaving Damian was for his own good and that he was better off without her.

But for some reason it sounded different this time. Like saying it aloud changed how she heard it, that it changed her a little. Maybe this really was closure. Maybe he would understand why she left and not hate her anymore for it.

"Nana told me my mom was dead. She'd died on the streets a few years before, out of her mind on drugs. She said she lost it in her early twenties and it was hereditary, and it would likely happen to me because I was just like my mother. She said the only reason she'd brought me in was because the state had given her a few hundred dollars a month to do so and that she wanted you to stay on the farm, but not me."

"Dammit, Kendall, that's horrible, but that's still not

enough! You didn't even talk to me about it."

"Like you didn't talk to me about Davis?" The accusation clearly hit home because he had the decency to look embarrassed. He *had* applied to the university and gotten into their program. And he hadn't told her. Obviously their bond, the one she'd believed in for so long, wasn't as strong as she'd thought. Maybe it had never had been.

"That's different. I didn't apply. My dad did. All I ever wanted was you. And this farm and our own family."

"But, don't you see, that's exactly what I couldn't give you. She didn't want me on this farm. More importantly, though, chances are I'm going to end up just like my mother. And my children, our children, could too!"

Kendall sat up and turned to him, waiting for it to sink in. Her family legacy of illness. The farm. Everything.

"You don't know that. Hell, you don't even know if she was telling the truth. Chances are she wasn't," he whispered to the ceiling. "You never even gave us a chance."

The agony in his voice coupled with the bottomless regret she felt tipped her over and the tears began to fall. "I couldn't do that to you. You deserve to be with someone whole. Someone who could give you healthy babies."

"So instead you did worse. You left me with nothing."

"You have the farm. And it's all yours...or it will be." Why couldn't he see what she'd done for him?

"None of it mattered without you. With you gone, I was just going through the motions."

She felt like he'd taken her heart and ripped it from her chest. "It means everything, Damian. Look what you've done. You're a genius. You turned this dirt patch into a thriving business and community. You make things, amazing things, and you employ people. Don't you see?" He was a natural, and in a time when farms were dying on the vine, he'd created one singlehandedly that was becoming more and more successful. "And, honestly, I wouldn't even ask you to share it with me—Lord knows I don't deserve even a little of it—if I wasn't so desperate."

"Bullshit. You deserve this farm far more than I do. It's your family legacy. It's all you have of any value from them."

She shook her head. No. Not true even in the slightest. Why couldn't she make him see that she left to save him from her? For all she knew, her epic and very public melt-down might be due to her inevitable mental deterioration.

"No, Damian," she said laying her hand on his check, wanting to get lost forever in the sandpapery rasp of his stubble and the hazelly green of his soulful eyes. "Nothing's changed. This belongs to you and I don't."

Chapter Seven

DAMIAN SLEPT VERY little before his phone alarm pulled him out of a bleary slumber at nearly five in the morning. After pulling Kendall into his arms and making love to her again, because he'd finally admitted to himself that's what it had been, *love*, he tucked her into his side and stroked her hair until her breaths grew deeper and evened out. He hadn't wanted to wake her after exhausting her both mentally and physically, so he'd done his tossing and turning in his head and not in the bed.

He loved his work on the farm, enjoyed the goats and even managing the shop and warehouse staff. But if he was ever going to take a morning off to lie around in bed it would be that very Monday morning. Before last night he had planned on teaching Kendall the ropes that day, but after her fall, their sexing, and then the emotional aftermath he decided to sneak out of bed and let her sleep.

Emerging from the en-suite bathroom, changed and groomed, he noticed the Kendall-sized indentation in his bed covers, but no Kendall. Making his way into the kitchen, he discovered her pouring coffee. Smiling almost shyly she handed him a steaming cup, along with a bowl of yogurt and some blueberries with granola.

"Still like your coffee black like an old man?" she teased. And he was struck, like a punch to his chest, at the yearning nostalgia that ran through him. This was the way it was, the way it was supposed to be, before everything went sideways.

"Still trying to kill me with your hippie food?" he teased back.

"Ironic coming from the goat-farming, soap-making dude with the beard and a flannel."

"What's that mean?"

"Hey, if the hipster farmer fits…"

He took a bite of his breakfast. "Ha. Ha."

She rinsed her bowl in the sink and set it in the dishwasher. "That granola is really good… Where'd you get it? It looks homemade."

"Delilah."

Her eyes widened in surprise. He knew she barely kept in touch with her former best friend. That Delilah had felt just as abandoned by Kendall as he had.

"She bought the old diner with her brother after Helena retired last year and moved to Montana to be with her niece's family."

"Oh," she said hiding her face and the blush he could see staining her cheeks. This time from embarrassment and not sex. But he left it at that, figuring he'd pushed her enough for one day. He let the silence settle in around them, enjoying the comfortable quiet and—though he didn't want to admit—her in his kitchen. After cleaning up her cup, Kendall moved to the front door and pulled on her boots.

He made a silent note to get them to town later that afternoon to buy her some proper farm boots. Although today, she should probably take it easy and stay in the house. As he was about to tell her exactly that she held up her hand and said, "Before you say anything, cowboy, forget it. I mean it. I'm here to help and that's what I'm going to do."

"First off, *cowgirl*, I'm the boss. Second, you hurt your ankle last night. One day off lounging around in the cabin isn't going to kill you, Kendall." He took the few steps toward her erasing the space between them and reached around her, watching her eyes widen and her pupils dilate until he grabbed his hat off the rack and plopped it on his head. "Sit your pretty little ass down on the couch. Drink coffee, read your books, and I'll be back later." And he left her staring open-mouthed after him as he turned and went out the front door, stomped down the steps, and made his way to the goat enclosure.

He shouldn't have been surprised that fewer than ten minutes later Kendall came up behind him and without a word started filling the feed receptacles and changing the water out for the goats.

"Kendall, I told you…"

Much to the chagrin of the five goats waiting to be fed she stopped scooping their food, and looked him straight in the eye, her chin jutting out as if preparing for a fight, and she pulled up her jeans to expose her wrapped ankle. It didn't appear swollen, but he did notice she was wearing running shoes and not boots. "I'm really okay. And I'll take it easy. I need to be out here, Damian. I promise I'll stop if my ankle hurts. I know you have no reason to believe me but try to trust me."

He stared at her face trying to ascertain what she was not telling him. Why was this so important to her? Why was she nearly begging him to believe her? Instead of asking, in the end he just nodded. "The minute you flinch or look like you're in pain I'm going to pick you up, throw you over my shoulder, and take you back to the cottage myself." Surprise swept across her features before she schooled them.

She chuckled, her voice low and smoky, much too sexy for five o'clock in the morning. "That's not really a threat, cowboy." She laughed again and turned back to her work, cooing to the mean old donkey and talking to the goats.

He watched her for a moment, struck again at how easily she fit into life on the farm. How easy it would be to forgive her and ask her to stay. But she probably wanted to get back on the road and play her music. Her life wasn't here any longer and the sooner he got that through his thick skull the better it would be for both of them.

The morning passed quickly, and Kendall showed a tenacious interest in all of the farm work Damian introduced her to—from cleaning out the milking stations to feeding the animals to harvesting the vegetables—and charmed all of his employees from the farmhands to the part-time college students who ran production and the shop. She showed special interest in how the different body products such as soaps and lotions were formulated and productized for distribution.

Damian was surprised at a couple of interesting marketing ideas Kendall put forth regarding selling his products on their website and rebranding the small shop at the front of the property. But of course, he shouldn't be surprised at her business savvy. She'd spent the last four years turning herself into a product and marketing machine. Everything with Kendall's punk rock cowgirl image was branding, branding, branding. She'd taken a wild child from the other side of the tracks with a penchant for singing and a talent for poetry and created a crossover star.

When a pair of battered and mud-covered shoes appeared in his vision as he pounded in the last nail on a broken fence enclosure, he looked up. Kendall stood above him with the midday sun blazing a golden halo bright against the clear sky. She looked angelic, like she did in his dreams some nights when he was too beat up and too exhausted to remember to hold on to his bitterness. He stood up and wiped the sweat and dirt from his forehead with the bottom of his shirt, not missing the burn of heat in her eyes or the way she bit down on the side of her lip.

She thrust a paper plate with a sandwich and cluster of

grapes, and a water bottle into his hands. "I brought you lunch." She shrugged her shoulder and looked almost shy as she glanced away and then back at him. "Thought you might be hungry."

He motioned to the back of the truck and pulled the gate down before hopping up. "Join me."

She shook her head, her hair shiny and in a loose braid. "I already ate."

"Sit anyway." He patted the spot next to him and she scooted up on the gate. Why was he making this harder on himself by pulling her closer and closer? It was time to figure out what the hell he was doing and how he could get himself to stop doing it. This woman was trouble. But after last night he wasn't sure he could go back to the way he had been. Not that he could fall back into being with Kendall again, but though he'd felt dead inside for years now, he realized he wasn't actually dead. And the more time he spent around her, the more alive he became.

But what did that mean for them? For him? He'd promised to buy her out, promised to give her the divorce she'd wanted for years. But what did he want? Aside from the anger, the bitterness, what did he want from her? He'd spent so many years yearning for her and then stewing in his own cynicism that he'd stopped thinking about what he wanted. Sure, he thought a lot about what had been and the future he felt Kendall had stolen from them. But he hadn't done a whole lot of thinking about now. Or the not-so-distant future.

He bit off a chunk of the ham and cheese sandwich and surveyed the land around him filled with goats, a large vegetable garden and covered greenhouse off to the right of the property. His two farmhands were moving a herd of goats from one field to another as a large brown delivery truck pulled to a stop in front of the entrance to the farm where the shop sat. Kelly Family Farms was a growing, successful, busy business. He'd loved farming from the first time he'd helped his mom in her kitchen garden after school, but really took to it after Kendall's grandma had hired him to work on the property the summer after his senior year in high school.

Once the next round of receivables cycled through he had plans to expand their product distribution a little further out, maybe hit some of the areas farther north up in Oregon where natural products were growing in popularity.

"Good?" Kendall's soft voice broke him out of his ruminations. "The sandwich…is it good?"

He smiled. "It's my favorite."

The edges of her glossy lips tipped up. She remembered.

Blowing out a long breath she leaned her head back and raised her face to the sun. "It smells so good out here. Like ocean and fresh grass and dirt. I forgot how much I missed it."

Her eyes snapped open like she hadn't meant to share that much. Hadn't meant to let him know she missed her home. Maybe even missed him.

It hit him like a bolt of lightning. A zing of electricity and a sudden sharp focus of energy. No matter how much she denied it, this *was* her home. She had gone out into the big bad world not because she'd wanted to become a super star, but because she'd felt she had no other choice but to leave and no other skills but singing and playing her guitar.

Kendall Kelly belonged in Blackberry Cove. That was the odd quiet that had settled over her since yesterday. Not sadness, but a calm that she probably hadn't felt since she left four years before. And hell if Damian had any idea what to do with that realization. So instead of dealing with it or even putting some space between the two of them, he opened his mouth and invited her to go on errands in town with him.

"You do realize that will start the gossip mill churning, don't you?" she asked with a mischievous smile.

He nodded. "Yep. But no more than me kissing you at the funeral, or you staying out here at the farm. Besides, woman, we're still married."

She hesitated and bit her lip for a moment before asking, "What about your dating...women...social life thing?"

Oh yeah. What about that, smartass? "Well, see, the thing is, my date with Carissa was really my first, well second date."

"In how long?"

He tapped his bottom lip and looked skyward. "Well, let's see, since you left...uhm, ever."

Her jaw dropped, and her eyes grew. "You mean…"

"Yep. One other date with a tourist but it didn't get farther than a good-night kiss on the cheek."

She mumbled something that sounded a lot like she hadn't dated either, which was obviously impossible. "What?"

"I said 'me too'," she said raising her voice only slightly then lifted her head from where she concentrated on her hands to peer up at him. "I haven't been with anyone else, Damian. I mean, guys tried, but I just couldn't. I'm still married."

"Yeah. Me, too."

"So last night."

He nodded. It had only ever been her. Those big brown eyes lifted and locked with his. And he felt like maybe his chest was filled with crushed glass and that the pieces were sliding around, slicing him up inside, making him raw, making him bleed. He felt exposed. Uncomfortable, but maybe, just maybe, those jagged edges might be smoothing out. Kendall might be sanding all that broken glass down into something softer and more manageable.

"Yeah." He reached over and brushed her long bangs off her forehead. Up close he could see the amber speckles in her eyes, the little dots that made her eyes glow and dance in the light. He cupped his hand over her jaw and smoothed his thumb along her bottom lip. She gasped, loud enough that he could hear it over the farm noise, but quiet enough that it was all for him. Like she had been and apparently still was. His.

God, he was such a selfish bastard.

"What are we doing?" she whispered, her voice almost a sigh.

"I don't know, sweetheart. I really don't know. How about we just go with it for the next couple weeks?"

"But what if you can't forgive me?" The desperation in her voice ate at him, made him want to kiss her fears away. But it wasn't that easy. Years of regret didn't just evaporate in one night or with something as simple as a kiss.

"But what if I can? What if you can forgive yourself?"

She shook her head and bit her lip. He tugged it free and leaned over to kiss her.

"Hey, boss," Coleman, one of the college kids who helped in the store, yelled from behind them. "Thomas from the farm store called. Your order is in." He stopped in front of the truck apparently oblivious to the sexual tension swirling around them, thick enough to reach out and pluck chunks of it out of the air. "You want me and Sam to run to town?" he asked referring to Samantha, the young woman responsible for mixing most of their body lotions and soaps. Just about everyone on the farm and nearly the entire town knew of Coleman Carter's crush on his childhood best friend, Samantha Villanueva. Everyone except Sam.

Damian hopped down from the truck and held his hand out to help Kendall down. "Nope. We were heading into town to pick up a few things anyway. Ready to go?"

"To town? Together?"

He nodded. She smiled, a real smile, the kind that lit up her brown eyes and everything else around her. "No time like the present to feed that rumor mill I suppose."

Chapter Eight

KENDALL WASN'T A pansy. She wasn't some country girl noob who didn't have any experience out in the real world. Well, she was, but she also had some hard-earned life experience to draw from. Hell, before being dumped on her grandmother at the age of ten she'd been bounced around from one foster home to another. One big fat ugly disappointment after the next had been her lot until ending up in Blackberry Cove.

Soon after realizing her grandma wasn't her fairy-tale family and that living with a bag packed and one foot out the door was probably the safest bet, she met Delilah Summerhill. Delilah split her time between her divorced parents: her mother in Blackberry Cove and her dad and his young wife and baby in Southern Oregon. And while both parents spent a great deal of time bickering about whose turn it was to keep Delilah they seemed far more interested in the fighting than they did their daughter.

Kendall and Delilah had forged strong bonds over subsidized school lunches and a healthy mix of alternative and country music. And when she'd run, she hadn't realized how much she'd actually left behind until it had been too late.

So when she walked into Big Al's Farm and Hardware Kendall found her eye drawn to the old diner across the street now painted a lively yellow and white with a wooden sign hanging above the door. "Delilah's." She felt a stab of regret and instead of pushing it away she let it cut through the years of denial. She stopped and wrapped her hand around Damian's wrist. "I'll meet you in there, okay?"

He nodded, obviously understanding that she had more work to do, more amends to offer. Because although she liked to live in her little hurt place where the only person she thought was really suffering was herself, she was beginning to understand that it wasn't nearly all that simple. That even her small pebble in the pond made bigger waves than she'd wanted to believe. And that perhaps it was time to own up to her martyrdom and fix the mess she'd left behind.

Kendall took a deep breath and smoothed her hands down her dusty jeans before shoving open the glass door to Delilah's, formerly the one and only cafe in Blackberry Cove's downtown strip, although now it appeared Otto's down the street was no longer just a bar but also a restaurant. She felt slightly unsettled walking into a place she'd never been welcome in when she'd lived here, since Helena had once accused her of stealing one of her dying potted plants in front of the café.

The bell rang over the door although none of the patrons seemed to pay her any attention as they continued their afternoon meals. A popular country song played over the sound system and the smells of good old-fashioned home-made country food filled the place. Delilah had transformed the place by ripping out the outdated and worn booths and replacing them with round wooden tables accented with colorfully painted mismatched chairs. Quirky art hung on the walls and one entire wall was painted in chalkboard paint and filled with menu items and funny sayings.

The diner really was Delilah's... Everything about it was her to a T.

Kendall raised her eyes to look over the small afternoon crowd, and though it felt like every single person in the entire county was suddenly staring at her, the truth was that maybe half a dozen couples glanced her way, of which she recognized two. Unfortunately, one of those couples hap-pened to be the former mayor of Blackberry Cove and her soon-to-be ex-father-in-law, Jonathan Sloane, sitting with his law partner, Joe McGreevy, the same attorney who had read Nana's will to her and Damian just days before. At the time Joe's distaste for her had been palpable. Although he'd never stepped out of line or said anything outright that could be construed as hurtful, Joe's dislike for her had been more than apparent. In a town full of people split evenly between those who despised Kendall and those who just blatantly ignored her, the two people at the top of the "Despises Kendall" list were glaring directly at her.

Great. Well, if the look on Mr. Sloane's face was any indication of his current feelings toward her she certainly wouldn't be stopping by their table and saying "hi" to her father-in-law any time soon. Although Joe wore a look of near boredom, like Kendall's appearance in the diner was dull and beyond his acknowledgment. Thankfully they were in the farthest booth away from the door and Kendall wouldn't have to include them in her walk of shame to Delilah.

Then she remembered who the hell she was—or at least who she pretended she was—and threw back her shoulders before walking to the counter where Delilah stood delivering an order. When she stood in front of her old friend unsure about whether to hug her or just slide into the booth, her friend surprised her with a frown.

"I'm still mad at you," was the first thing out of Delilah's mouth.

Normally, Kendall's go-to response would be to brush the comment off with a snarky comeback or a flippant distraction, but for some reason she seemed to be out of witty responses and casual shrugs. For some reason, she let her fake public smile drop, the one colored matte red with her favorite lip stain, and she leaned up to wrap her arms around Delilah, who happened to be significantly taller than Kendall. Delilah's body felt stiff for a full moment before she softened and pulled her into a giant hug.

"I'm sorry, Delilah. For everything," Kendall said simply, closing her eyes. Perhaps there'd be time to clear away the cobwebs of the lonely past. Perhaps not. Nevertheless, she wanted Delilah to know how truly sorry she was that when she'd walked away from this town she hadn't just left Nana and Damian behind, she'd also left behind the one important friendship she'd ever cultivated...then or now. And even on her quick trips back to town when her grandma had insisted she come back for whatever non-existent reason, she hadn't called Delilah. From shame. From regret. From misguided fear. And suddenly it made her that much wearier.

Up until now she'd carried the weight of losing Damian, her sister's death, the plummeting to earth of her career, the passing of her grandmother, and even being stuck back in Blackberry Cove fairly well. At least to the discerning eye she still looked like she held some of her shit together. But the heaviness of it all was becoming too much. Maybe it was time to share the burden with someone else. Maybe if she'd trusted Damian, or even Delilah, all those years ago she wouldn't be such a hot mess now.

She opened her eyes to see Mr. Sloane and his partner sitting with pinched looks, but at least they were pretending to ignore her. So there was that. They could all pretend their pasts weren't intertwined, but their linked history in this town was undeniable. From the public humiliation of the Sloanes making it essentially illegal for Kendall to attend her senior prom with her husband to her final conversation with Mr. Sloane on the porch of the cottage she shared with

Damian. To the lawyers' rude oversight of Nana's will. Their hatred for her had deeper roots in this town than she did. But they'd won. The Sloanes always won.

Turning away she pulled back from Delilah and slid into the closest empty booth. Her friend grabbed Kendall's hand and squeezed it and scooted in next to her. "Tammy, can you cover me for a minute?" she yelled over her shoulder at an older red-haired waitress who nodded. "Sorry I couldn't make it to the ceremony," she said to Kendall.

They both laughed since Nana had made no secret of her dislike of anyone, but she'd been especially vocal about "that trollop Delilah," though she'd never been quite clear about what exactly made Delilah a trollop, or what the hell a trollop was. Kendall just assumed Nana's dislike was purely a reaction to her being Kendall's friend. She'd even disliked Damian until he proved he could care for both women and the property they shared while going to school at the local college. Nana's intense dislike of humans in general could be overlooked in lieu of their value to her. And Damian worked his ass off; therefore he had a lot of value.

"Well, you always were her favorite." Kendall smiled and placed her other hand on Delilah's. "Seriously though. I just had to go, Del." She was surprised to hear the crack in her voice and was more than just a little afraid that little crack might turn into a giant fissure that would grow and finally break her apart…right here in front of half the citizens of Blackberry Cove.

"I know, sweetie. You tried to explain it in the email. And, believe it or not, I got it. Even the parts you left out."

"Left out?" She hadn't omitted the part where Jonathan Sloane had threatened to disown his son completely if she didn't promptly exit his life. Although she had been too full of shame to tell her about her mom's mental illness. Though now she was beginning to feel like maybe fear was a better description. It hadn't been her poor mom's fault. And maybe if she'd had the support of her own mother she might have had a better shot at life. Well, she wasn't going to dwell on that now.

"You know, the truth part." Delilah raised her perfectly shaped brows. "Oh you look surprised that we could be friends from the age of ten and I would know the real reason you left."

"I…uhm…I don't know what you mean."

"Oh, I'm sure you do, Kendall," Delilah prompted but sat still. Waiting.

An itchy panic began to slither over her skin and rumble in her belly. "I left because I was in over my head. I left because no one wanted me here any longer. I left because I was ruining Damian's life. I left to play music…"

Delilah slapped her free hand on to the table, drawing glances from the diners at the table across from them. "Stop it. Just stop it. So many excuses and not one of them the truth."

Panic turned to shock, a sharp stab of anger mixed with

fear. She wasn't ready for this conversation. Not now…who knows, maybe not ever. And what did it matter? What was done was done. The past. Really nothing good would come from the truth. In fact it could make everything so much worse. The past was too broken to fix.

"Why do you insist on letting everyone think you're a monster?"

"Why do you think I care what everyone thinks about me?" Somehow she managed to straighten her spine and angle her head in a manner she knew from endless photo shoots lent her an air of coolness, of confidence. The whole town had already thought nothing of her. Or they thought the worst. "Best let them have their little fantasies, don't you think?"

"No, I don't think. What I believe is that you left because your evil grandma finally dug her nails into you too hard. And I think that somehow the Sloanes, or Damian's dad at the very least, convinced you that leaving their son, the love of your life, would be better for him."

Heat crawled up her neck and tightened around her throat. The room felt uncomfortably warm, the laughter around her forced. Even the clinking of glasses and forks on plates seemed somehow hollow and sad.

"Please don't," Kendall whispered. "Please…"

"Kendall. When will it stop? The martyrdom of Kendall Kelly has to end at some point. And the truth seems so much easier, so much less painful. Haven't you both suffered enough? I mean, unless this is your thing." Delilah smirked and took a sip of the water Tammy had set on their table.

"I told him everything." Kendall wanted to duck her head and hide her eyes from her perceptive friend. But she didn't. Damian and Delilah were right. She owed them, everyone, the truth about why she left. It wouldn't change anything, couldn't fix what she'd already ruined, but it might ease the move forward. For everyone.

"What is everything, Kendall?" Delilah asked, and pulled both of Kendall's hands under hers.

Kendall had explained to Delilah the night she left, in her letter, how both Mr. Sloane and her grandmother had ripped her up and thrown her out. How she'd feared they were right, that she'd never be good enough for Damian, and that she'd probably follow in her mother's footsteps. The thought of ruining his life and Damian never being a father had crushed her. She'd known he would have dismissed her fears, but she couldn't let him make that choice. So she'd made it for him.

"First off, honey, you are still as full of shit as you always were. I mean, I love you. I do. But that man has been nothing but miserable without you. And what about you?"

"What about me?"

"How's that music career working out?"

"Not so good. My business manager ran off with my recording advance. My record company canceled my contract and wants the money back. I'm staying just as long as it takes for Damian to buy me out and then I can pay the money back."

"Then what? You running away again?"

"As much as I wish I could stay with Damian, it's not meant to be. I hate this place and it hates me. I need to move on." And it was true. No matter how much her heart ached for a life with her husband, everything she'd done and said had been true. She'd never be happy here and she couldn't give him the life he deserved.

"Well maybe you need to stop making decisions for everyone else and stop running from yourself. You might see Blackberry Cove in a different light." She shrugged and pulled herself from the booth. Before Kendall could process her comment, let alone respond, Delilah leaned over and kissed her on her cheek. "Let's go out Saturday night. Have dinner at Otto's and maybe a couple drinks and some dancing."

It was on the tip of Kendall's tongue to decline. She was feeling a bit overexposed right at that moment and wasn't sure she was ready to put herself out there, in front of the entire town, for evisceration. But to her surprise she nodded. She missed her friend, missed that connection to another person with shared history. Someone she'd known for years and knew all her baggage. "Sure," she said. "I'll meet you there at nine this Saturday."

Delilah smiled. "There she is. My old friend—welcome back." Then she turned and went to the front of the diner, greeting a couple that had just walked in.

DAMIAN PRETENDED TO take great interest in the various shovels in front of him. It was strictly coincidental that the display gave him a clear shot of the front door of the farm and hardware store. Or that's what he repeatedly told himself when his gaze swung to the glass doors that Kendall finally walked through nearly forty minutes after leaving him to see Delilah.

Kendall's long blonde and pink hair was braided and hung down her back like a beautiful woven rope. She still wore those muddy sneakers, and had changed into a clean pink T-shirt and worn but clean jeans. As she looked around the warehouse store, presumably looking for him, she was stopped by the oversolicitous son of the store owner who leaned in to her a little too closely and smiled a little too widely. Damian took a step toward them but stopped abruptly, remembering that she was no longer his and she had no intention of sticking around even if he got down on his knees and begged her to stay. And he'd never do that.

Would he? Of course not.

But why not? She obviously ran because she'd been frightened of his father and of her possible future medical issues. But weren't those just excuses? If she'd talked to him, told him what had happened, she knew well enough he'd have dismissed her fears and assured her of his love. Too bad it was too late.

Why? Was it really too late? What if she could fall back in love with him?

And what if he could forgive her for everything? Could he ever trust her again? Or would he just walk around waiting for the other shoe to drop? He shook his head and mumbled *idiot* under his breath.

From across the way he watched the clerk point to him as Kendall turned, locking her gaze with his. She waved and smiled, bouncing on her toes. That big, beautiful all Kendall Kelly grin nearly brought him to his knees. Before he could stop it, an answering smile transformed his face and his legs moved him toward her. She met him halfway and wrapped her arms around his waist.

"She forgave me, Damian." Kendall's voice was low and breathless. Her eyes were shiny. "How could I have been so wrong?"

Impulsively he bent down and kissed her cheek. "About what, Kendall?" he asked feigning nonchalance. Did she mean him too?

She mumbled something. Something that sounded a lot like the word everything. But instead of repeating it like he wanted her to—and he was seconds away from begging her to do just that—she buried her head in his chest and squeezed his waist tightly. Maybe she wasn't quite ready to make that kind of definitive statement. And he sure as hell wasn't ready to hear it. So he buried his nose in her hair and kissed her behind her ear.

A throat clearing behind them forced him to look up. They were literally standing in the middle of the front of the store hugging and nearly kissing. If they had wanted to keep their new-old weird relationship or lack thereof on the down low, it wasn't happening. Because standing behind them was Mr. Fallbrook, gossip king of Blackberry Cove.

Kendall and Damian untangled themselves and stood facing the biggest busybody in two counties. "Heard you were stuck in town until Damian here could buy you out. Didn't hear that you two were back at it."

"Hello, Mr. Fallbrook. How are you? How's your grandson?" Kendall asked. The old man's face turned red and then a frightening plum color.

"He's just fine. Off at school. You stay away from him!"

"Why, Mr. Fallbrook, I'm a married woman. Besides I can't help it if he followed me around like a puppy dog."

Damian hid his chuckle behind a well-timed cough, remembering John Fallbrook and how the young teen called Kendall and asked her out nearly every day. Once going so far as ordering her an expensive bike online—using his grandfather's credit card—and offering it as a birthday present. His heart tightened at the memory of Kendall pushing that bike back to his house, holding John's hand as he cried his undying devotion to her. She could have been so cruel and unkind like the all the kids of Blackberry Cove had been to her.

But that wasn't Kendall.

Kendall had softened the first break of a young teen's heart with compassion and true friendship. Even if John had ended up turning on her, which he had eventually when he'd boasted to his friends that he'd slept with Kendall at a party she hadn't even attended. Damian had just started dating her and decided then and there that he would be her champion, her support, her backup. She was strong, she looked after herself and those she thought needed her help, but no one except Delilah had her back. His woman hit rock bottom and still came up swinging. But when she didn't he was always there to help her back up. And quietly punish those who hurt her.

His woman. Dammit. He really was going back down that path, wasn't he?

Damian interrupted whatever sputtering cruelty was on the tip of the old man's razor tongue. "Quit harassing my wife, Fallbrook. Maybe you should work on keeping your side of the street clean, buddy, before shoving your nose in ours."

Patting Kendall's ass and then grabbing her hand, he pushed her toward the building and lumber section at the back of the large warehouse store, leaving the cranky old man to stew in his own unhappiness.

"The wood section, Damian?" She smirked, her lips so pink and full. "Are you trying to tell me something?"

Grabbing her by the shoulders, he spun her into a hidden corner and pushed her against the wall. Her little gasp, followed by a low sigh, caught in his mouth and settled in his chest as he wrapped one hand around her jaw, spread the other across her back between her hot body and the wall, and lowered his mouth onto hers. Soft. Familiar. Oddly new. This weird neediness he had for her since seeing her sitting in the church just a few days before turned into something softer. Something bigger. Something he still wasn't ready to name. So he put it all into the kiss.

For a minute, he let his sullenness go—letting it turn to smoke and drift away—and imagined they could be together. For more than just now. For later. Forever.

Forever.

Slowly he pulled back from her to look down into her face. Her eyes were open, staring at him with some unknown emotion. The moment was too heavy with the past and the unknown and the hurt and the desire. So thick in the air between them he feared it would suffocate them both.

"The wood is for the porch. And new floors for the main house," he said and then he dipped his hips and ground his erection into her, smiling when her eyes dilated and her lids dropped. "And that wood is for you. Later."

"What happened to one and done, cowboy?" she teased.

"Not enough." And it hadn't been. His gut was telling him it would never be enough. But he wasn't listening to that shit. Not just yet.

She smiled and didn't push. Thankfully. "Okay. So floors?" She moved away from his body and stood in front of the flooring chart. He moved to stand next to her.

"The upstairs floors are in pretty good shape. Some sanding and staining should bring them back to life," he said. "But the downstairs isn't salvageable in some areas and then the carpet in other areas is plain gross. Might as well replace it all."

She nodded, still looking at the choices. "These are all nice."

"But…"

"But nothing. They're pretty. Which do you like best?"

"This way." He steered her to the very back where piles of different planks of varying lengths and beautiful shades of brown were stacked.

Kendall brought her hands together in a quiet clap. "Reclaimed barn wood." She smiled and looked up at him. Damian nodded. "You remembered."

"Everything."

"Me too," she whispered and turned to him. "I remember everything, Damian."

Chapter Nine

THE REST OF the week passed quickly. Too quickly for Kendall's liking. Because once the farm's receivables came in and Damian could buy her out, she would have her money and be on her way to pay back her label. Just like they'd agreed. She still didn't know where since she'd avoided thinking about the future, or even beyond the moment, so that she could throw herself into every second she had with Damian on the farm. But the hard and rewarding work during the day nearly always ended with them on the cottage porch, Kendall picking at her guitar and Damian sipping a beer. Sometimes she sang and he listened. Sometimes they talked. And every night she went to bed next to Damian with something raw and broken in her chest. Something that felt an awful lot like longing for the farm. For Blackberry Cove. For Damian. For home.

The downstairs floors in her grandmother's house had been transformed quickly with the help of the farm staff and had gone in even faster when Damian hired a contractor to mill and plane the reclaimed wood, and then installed it. Damian and Kendall had sanded it before Damian stained it.

By Saturday, he was on the second coat of stain and Kendall couldn't believe how new floors could make the old house come back to life.

By Saturday night Kendall wanted nothing more than to curl up in bed next to Damian in his cottage, which she'd never left after the night she'd hurt her ankle, and read a romance novel or watch a movie. But that was the night she'd promised to have dinner with Delilah. And though she looked forward to spending time with her old friend she'd had some reservations about exposing herself to the towns-people again. Walking into Otto's alone was tantamount to walking through the town square buck naked. An idea that did not appeal to her in any way whatsoever.

But she was used to doing everything on her own. And this was no different. Nor was it something special. Really, how difficult was it to go out to dinner with a friend, and maybe do a little dancing? Hell, she should be happy she could do that here without some asshole photographer trying to get a photo under her dress or provoke her into saying something stupid on video. She wasn't exactly anonymous in Blackberry Cove, but she was, at least, a little less notorious.

When she walked out of the cottage's bathroom after putting the final touches on her hair and makeup, Damian was lounging on the bed with his hands behind his neck and his long legs crossed at the ankles. The look on his face was dark...not quite angry, but ferocious all the same.

"You know, cowboy, if that were my bed, I'd kick you to

the curb for putting your boots on the comforter."

Swinging his legs down to the floor, he reached out and placed his hands on her hips. "You look crazy fucking sexy in these leather pants." He leaned forward and kissed her belly on the exposed swath of skin that wasn't covered by her low-slung pants or her "country girl" T-shirt.

"Don't worry, I'm going to put on a big floppy sweater," she said pointing to the long red, ruffled garment she'd left on the bed.

"I'm not worried." Her body shuddered as he ran his tongue just above the edge of her pants, essentially melting anything hard or jagged in her body for good. His hands ran up and under the hem of her shirt until they palmed her lace-covered breasts. She leaned in to him as a warm, liquid feeling pulsed at the apex of her thighs.

"No?" She gasped the word.

"You know you belong to me, don't you, sweetheart?" His mouth moved to her left breast, and bit sharply at the hardened bud there, mouthing her through the cotton material. "Everyone knows, don't they?"

The shudder turned to a tremble. Her whole body ached and wanted and needed. Another bite to her other nipple stole her response so she answered with a nod. To deny their connection, their hold on each other, would be a lie. And she was done lying.

Kendall finally gathered her waning energy and wrapped her hands around his head, angling his face up so she could

KASEY LANE

see his beautiful eyes. "But that goes both ways, doesn't it?"

His lips quirked up and his eyes went from beautiful to mesmerizing, hypnotic. "Baby, what are we going to do?"

She hadn't meant to sound so achingly hollow. But it was there…in her tone. And he heard it but kept that smile and bit at her belly before letting her go. She knew he'd overheard part of her call from the record label that morning when they'd been feeding the goats. He hadn't asked her about it yet and she hadn't shared the content of the discussion. She would, but first she had to process it.

"That all depends, doesn't it?" he said, handing her the sweater.

"On what?"

He stood and kissed her cheek. "On whatever it is you have going on up there in that fast-moving brain of yours."

"We'll talk about it. Not now—" she glanced at her phone and stepped into her black-heeled knee boots "—but soon."

He nodded, almost curtly, a sharp quick motion that succinctly ended that portion of the conversation.

"I'd like to drive you tonight. I'm going to meet my mom for dinner." He laughed. "Don't look so surprised. Maybe it's time to mend some fences."

"I'm really glad." And she was. Dr. Sloane had been so obviously pained and remorseful that Kendall had felt sorry for her. Besides, it had been Mr. Sloane who had been so cruel that night. She'd only assumed that his wife agreed with his involvement. But that appeared to not be the case. "But you don't have to drive me."

"I want to. I can drop you off, have dinner with my mom, and pick you up. If you're not ready, I'll just have a beer at the bar." He said it like this was a normal thing. A husband dropping off and picking up his wife. And she wished it was—God she wished it so much. But that wasn't their relationship and he didn't have to play that role.

He reached out and wrapped his fingers around her wrist, gently stroking the underside. Shivers ran up her arm…but, hey, what else was new? Every time Damian touched her, her skin went on high alert. "It's okay. And, it's probably a win-win if you want me to pick you up earlier," he said leaving out the real reason she might end the night early, which would be that it did not go well, or she ran into someone who might say or do something hurtful.

He was right, though. The night could go south quickly. It was nice to have him on her side. Even if it was just temporary she would take it. She'd take just about anything he was willing to give.

Kendall reached up and kissed him on his cheek, loving the rough texture of his stubble against her lips. Moving his head, he turned the sweet peck into a sensual and suggestive dance of tongues. When he finally pulled away they were both breathless.

"Well it's a good thing I'm wearing lip stain, cowboy." She laughed, not liking the nervous lilt of her voice. She was getting in too deep with him. Again. And it was going to hurt more than ever when she had to walk away.

And once she told him about the call from the label, he'd be more than ready to wipe his hands clean of her and their relationship. But for right now she desperately wanted to hold on to the moment, this one right here, with him.

Because the moment she started thinking she might actually already be home, Kendall would remember the call, remember what she owed, and how badly she'd hurt her husband. And that dream, the one of living here in Blackberry Cove and being a real wife to her husband would drift away.

She had to tell him about the call. Just not yet.

WHEN SHE SWANNED in promptly at nine, Kendall was shocked at how full the room was. If Blackberry Cove could possibly experience something as modern as gentrification, then perhaps the once-notorious bar and grill had been caught up in a renaissance because instead of cheap, torn, and mismatched plastic chairs and tables it now featured a modern steel and wood bar across one side of the Victorian warehouse-like building. Plush dark blue booths lined the outside edge of the room, lending an impression of privacy, although it was more likely that the raised booths were where one sat if they wanted to see and be seen. Most of the booths and the tables sprinkled throughout the room were full of people as was the dance floor before the stage on the farthest side of the large room.

The second she walked in she was instantly considering her options for flaking on the one person in town who still might actually like her. The impulsive decision to meet her at what was apparently the most popular place in town had been foolish. Since Kendall was not interested in exposing her throat to the wildlife of the town any more than she already had. Thankfully, Damian had seen her anxiety and she felt much better, more settled just knowing he'd be coming back for her.

And, really, all she wanted to do after the ridiculously hard, but still kind of fun, day on the farm was go to bed…and not dream about her soon-to-be ex-husband and his tanned, sinewy forearms or the way they bulged and pulsed as he dug post holes or unloaded hay from the back of the farm truck. Or the way her heart sang and then sunk every time her gaze would collide with his.

Though they'd had sex several times since that first night, it had been more a frantic combustion of pent-up lust, and perhaps a need to christen every damn surface in the cabin, than a communion of their souls. Maybe that was because they had a lot of lost time to make up. Or maybe it was the sheer exhaustion of working a farm every day. Either way, she couldn't help wondering if it was something else. Something having to do with Damian keeping her at a distance. Which made sense, right? She was leaving, and he didn't want it to screw up his whole world again. And though she desperately wanted more from Damian, how could he trust his heart to her again. After how she'd left? But she'd had reasons, right? Real reasons to protect him from a shaky future.

Or were they really just more excuses to keep her from more heartache? Had she left because she feared he'd eventually leave her like everyone else had? The realization was a kick to her stomach. But when her friend called to her across the room she chose to shove that feeling down. Way down.

"Hey, girl, over here." Delilah waved, her short black bob straight and glossy under the low lights, and called across the noisy crowd. So much for a stealthy entrance or an even stealthier exit. "Kendall!" Delilah called again from a corner booth and Kendall felt a number of eyes turn and glare at her. Yep, this had definitely been the wrong decision. So, so, so wrong for so many reasons.

Delilah looked stunning as usual in a short flowing skirt and tight corset-style top that complemented her high cheekbones and bronze skin tone.

Kendall hugged her friend and they slid into the booth, both pretending to ignore the attention their little get-together was attracting from the other patrons.

"Stop looking so…so mad," Delilah said before hiding her smirk behind a sip of her cranberry-colored drink. "Unless that's still your thing."

"My thing?" Kendall squeaked.

"Yeah. You know, you like being hated or whatever. The tragic, unloved Kendall Kelly of Blackberry Cove. The whole sadly romantic notion of star-crossed lovers and all that."

The acidic ribbon coiled tighter in her body. Kendall didn't trust her voice so she shook her head. That was so not true.

Or was it?

"Really? So you're happy then? Awesome, shall we toast to your success?" Delilah raised her glass in mock celebration.

Thankfully the waiter interrupted and took their order, which bought Kendall a few minutes to silence her galloping heartbeat and figure out her exit strategy. She loved Delilah and had missed her, so much more than she'd realized until her friend had wrapped her in a real hug, but she wasn't ready for this heart-to-heart. She suspected that once they started talking about her precarious life situation then the whole mess of self-deceiving lies she'd built her life on would turn to dust and she'd have nothing left to hide behind.

But before she could formulate her exit, the waiter turned from the table revealing a tall, blonde, very attractive woman.

"Hello, Carissa," Delilah said coolly. "I'm sure you remember Kendall." The other woman smiled. A sort of vicious slash on her sculpted, beautiful face.

"Of course. How odd to see you here still, Kendall. I

thought you'd be long gone by now. I'm sure you've heard I'm dating your ex-husband," she said, the words hitting their intended mark, sliced through her center leaving her feeling raw and exposed.

"You mean my *husband*." Kendall smiled back, as cheerfully as if she were on a press junket, not giving Carissa a chance to see her bleed.

Carissa's face reddened. "*Ex*-husband," Carissa said again. Kendall had spent the last few years on stage or in front the camera, and she couldn't bear to let go a situation so ripe with drama. So she paused. For one, two, three beats. She waited until nearly everyone in the restaurant had predictably stopped talking and turned to glare at her.

"No, honey. We're still very married."

They all hated her. She knew that. Once Kendall had realized her efforts to charm the people of Blackberry Cove had failed, she'd done practically everything in her power to ensure they'd have reason to dislike her. So why did she taunt Damian's would-be date? Why did it matter anymore? Especially when he was sharing her bed—or vice versa—and she'd be gone soon enough anyhow.

"That's a lie," Carissa croaked. "He divorced your ass years ago."

"Did he actually tell you that, Carissa?" Kendall asked and watched the other woman's face dropped when she realized she'd assumed, just like everyone else in town, that Damian and Kendall had legally ended their marriage.

Kendall snagged Damian's gaze as he walked up behind Carissa. His face looked cold and passive, but his beautiful hazel eyes glowed green so he was either livid or turned on. Somehow she doubted he was feeling passionate as his potential new girlfriend and estranged wife paired off.

Kendall stared at her husband, the only man she'd ever loved, admiring his dark hair combed back and his black barely there beard neatly trimmed. He wore a blue and black plaid western shirt rolled up at the sleeves to reveal insanely muscled forearms, the same ones that had driven her crazy all day, tucked into low-hung jeans. Goddamn, that man was fine. She'd been all over the country and met models, actors, and musicians that the commercial world considered smoking hot and not one of them even came close to him. Not one. Ever.

Slowly the side of his mouth curved into that wildly sexy smile of his. That little bend did crazy things to her insides, flooding her with images of him in bed that morning. This man had always held too much power over her. Even when he was standing next to another woman she couldn't look away from the intensity that shone from his every pore.

"Yes, Carissa, Kendall is still my wife." Damian's voice was deep and crystal clear. And when he leaned down to hand Kendall her purse—the one she must've left in his truck—he pressed his mouth to hers in a provocatively lingering kiss, leaving no doubt in anyone's mind that he was claiming her once again. She should push him away. One gentle shove to his chest and he'd back off. It would save them both a lot of trouble in the end.

But she couldn't. Dammit. She wouldn't. That feeling of belonging to someone, to him, of knowing that he would have her back came flooding over her. It was overwhelming. She was drowning in him. Here in public. But her hand came up to cup his jaw, to rub her thumb across the long stubble there, to luxuriate in the moment of being Damian's once again.

He pulled back and smiled at her before standing. "Hello, wife."

Chapter Ten

DAMIAN SAID THE word *wife* without the usual discomfort weighing down his tongue. Yes, he still wanted to punish Kendall for leaving him, for ruining his life, but he continued to hold her gaze with his own and couldn't bring himself to provide her with more public humiliation than she'd already lived through in Blackberry Cove. Could he forgive her? Maybe. Regardless, his role as her protector from the rest of the world was ingrained bone deep, as much a part of him as his own personality.

Aw hell.

Damian was getting lost in Kendall again. When she calmed and then melted under his rough touch he felt centered. Right. The feel of his mouth on hers. Her fingers gripping his jaw. The tightness in his chest turned from uncomfortable to…to home. This is where she belonged. With him. He needed her to want him, to need him, to love him again. They were meant for each other.

They always had been.

A fork dropped, and a patron laughed somewhere, pulling him out of his Kendall-induced daydream. Obviously

Otto's was not the place to have this life-determining realization. Regretfully, he pulled back and stood next to Carissa.

"What?" Carissa shrieked. "You're still married?" she asked again. "I thought you were divorced. When are you getting divorced?"

Delilah stood from her seat and started to move toward Carissa. "Hey, you have no…"

"I apologize, Carissa," Damian said stepping between his…his whatever Carissa was and Delilah. "Kendall and I are still married. Not really your business—"

"You apologize? Why did you ask me out if you're still married to her? She left you!" Carissa's fair skin was turning a dangerous reddish purple and she was starting to make a scene. He could feel a dozen sets of eyes burning into the back of his neck. But he ignored them, just like he had for the last several years, both before and after Kendall left.

Why the hell had he asked her out?

Maybe you wanted to make Kendall jealous.

Ridiculous of course. Completely coincidental that he'd suggested dinner the day he saw Carissa in town before the memorial service. The service he knew his wayward wife would be attending.

"I'm sorry. I don't have…" Kendall began, quietly, from her seat, suddenly looking so young and uncomfortable. "I don't…it's not…"

"Don't," he said without thinking to Kendall, but before

she could argue with him, which she looked all set to do with her jaw tight and her eyes scrunched up, he turned to Carissa. "This is done. You need to go."

Carissa was still going on about Kendall as he directed her back to her friends at the end of the bar. What was she doing here? Why were they still married? When was she leaving? Was she staying with him on the farm? Endless questions, but never bothering to wait for answers. And Damian was approaching his limit on Carissa's prattle, and moved to the other end of the bar.

He glanced at his watch. The music would get louder and the patrons wilder the second the lights dimmed at 10:01. Kendall and Delilah had just enough time to eat dinner and get the hell out of there before Carissa went ballistic again or one of his dad's cronies decided tonight was the night to make a big move.

He ordered a beer and stepped into the hall to call his mom, promising to call her the next day to reschedule their dinner. Then he texted Kendall, letting her know he'd be hanging out there, but staying out of her hair. Leaving Kendall on her own clearly wasn't an option and she deserved to have a fun night out with her friend without some asshole hassling them. When he walked back into the main room from the hall Kendall looked up from her phone and waved, an open, happy smile on her face. He winked at her and made his way to back to the bar.

The bartender, Brian, a new farm employee who cared

for the goats and helped out with the shipping of their goat milk products during the day, slid him a dewy bottle. He tipped his chin and asked, "Will I see you tomorrow?"

The kid blushed, probably remembering the uncomfortable conversation they'd had the month before when Brian had shown up for work with bright red eyes and smelling like a distillery. Damian had talked to him about responsibility and sent him home looking shell-shocked. Since then he'd picked up a second job working weekends at Otto's and hadn't been late once, let alone shown up still reeking of the night before.

"Yes, sir." Brian looked him in the eye and stood tall. A boy becoming a man right before his very eyes.

They discussed the big order they had to fill in the next couple days and chatted about the memorial while Damian sipped his beer and glanced over at Delilah and Kendall's table where two dude bros he'd gone to high school with had joined them. He cursed under his breath and glowered in their direction.

But what the hell did he care? He didn't. He didn't give a shit when she smiled at the guy sitting next to her and laughed when he leaned over and said something in her ear. He didn't even care when her eyes shot to his as she stood up and walked toward the stage.

He certainly didn't care when she took the shiny red guitar from Colin, Otto's son and the current owner of the fancy new and improved Otto's.

But he did care when Brian asked, "What's Ms. Kelly doing up there?"

"OTTO'S IS EXCITED to offer some evening entertainment from the one and only local girl, the punk rock cowgirl herself, Kendall Kelly!" Colin Maslow, the town's former bad boy, said into the microphone. He'd been enthusiastically insistent when he'd recognized Kendall, rushing up to the table and hauling her into a warm hug.

Delilah had been less than pleased when Colin had wrapped her in his long, well-muscled arms before she extricated herself with a growl. Colin had responded with a laugh and turned his attention back to Kendall. Eventually his charisma and tenacity had won and she'd begrudgingly stepped onto the stage.

The polite smattering of applause his announcement elicited was anemic at best, but Kendall swallowed down her discomfort and willed herself to not look at any recognizable faces in the restaurant or any of the bemused or outright belligerent expressions peering up at her. Not Carissa and her group of friends who hadn't stopped glaring at her since she'd walked in, and certainly not her husband who looked up at her from his spot at the bar with an intense, but inscrutable expression. This was her domain, the one place she felt in control and at ease. Or it had been once upon a time. The stage.

The lights blurred out the faces in the restaurant giving her the absurd feeling of anonymity in a room full of people. Possibly hostile people. It made it so much easier to don her punk rock cowgirl persona. On stage she was KENDALL KELLY...and she owned it. Usually. Although this was different. So, so, so very different.

She swallowed down the dust in her throat and took a sip of water from the bottle Colin handed her. Setting it down, she pulled herself to her full height and cleared her throat before tugging the guitar strap over her head. The usual rush of adrenaline that washed through her when she stepped onto any stage, making her feel both drugged and grounded, never came. Instead she just felt dry and exposed. What great luck to suddenly feel like she was chewing on boulders seconds before singing in front of her hometown crowd. She said a silent "thank you" to the universe that she'd put on her fitted leather pants and sleek high-heeled black boots. Simple. Not trashy. Nothing to draw too much attention, or even more, too much criticism.

Delilah sat at their table with her hands clasped together and a huge smile dominating her lovely face. Nothing would quell the pounding of Kendall's heart against her ribcage, but having a friend in the room helped. How long had it been since she'd been on stage and looked over to see someone who wanted something good for her other than their commission? At least a couple months, and it had been over a month since her record fell off the lists and her tour was canceled along with her recording contract. But it felt like a lifetime. Even the man sitting across the room who had once sworn to love her until death was barely warming up to her. She could feel Damian's eyes on her, but was too much of a coward to meet his gaze.

So she looked at Delilah. Her friend. And she leaned into the moment. No more running from the here and now. She breathed in, allowing the sizzling energy in the air to fill her lungs, the acidic boil in her belly to fuel her, and the sheer thrill of creating music be the magic that it always was. She ran her fingers down the neck of the guitar and felt out the strings, fiddling with the tuning, loving the bite of the metal pressing into her still-calloused fingertips.

"Hi. I'm sure you all are thrilled to see me back in town, right?" She laughed, at herself and at this mean little town. That was something she was pretty good at. Hell, she'd spent nine years here laughing at herself, trying to make everyone else around her feel comfortable by constantly playing the fool to her own jokes. Old habits died hard. "Colin asked me to sing a couple songs so I'm gonna do that. You go ahead and eat your dinner and drink your drinks. Don't mind me."

The bright dinner lights dimmed, throwing a soft glow over the room and spotlight over the stage, and she felt her smile stretch across her face like it had a million times before: wide, bright, fake. But no one else needed to know that, she thought, until she caught Damian's enigmatic stare. And once again it was a punch to the gut the way his greenish brown eyes dug into hers, like they still owned her heart, her soul. But they didn't because she was pretty sure he didn't want her like she wanted him. Pretty sure she was still on her own.

Kendall wrenched her gaze away from his and closed her eyes. She wasn't here for him. She wasn't here in this moment on this stage to make amends. She was here for herself, wasn't she? She was here to finally bury the past and figure out some kind of future for herself. She was here to sing because that was what she was good at even if she wasn't good at the business of it.

Her fingers slid across the steel strings of the guitar and found their position as she began to strum the opening chords to a not-so-popular ballad from a very popular male county star, a hauntingly simple song about longing and the inevitability of loneliness after losing the love of one's life. Kendall could feel the notes move through her hands and merge with her body's sparking energy as her voice soared and she began to felt light and airy, like she always did when she sang. She felt transparent, yet wholly anchored for the few moments she was allowed to create art with her voice and guitar. For just a short while, she had value. She mattered and wasn't just surviving or going through the motions or running from the press or even struggling to create new songs. For now she just made magic from air.

She sang to the chorus, not exactly hating the cracked

huskiness of her voice and the way it echoed through the room. Opening her eyes she was almost surprised to see the room full of diners enjoying her music, and not actually throwing their artsy brew or avocado toast or whatever they ate in this new hipsterish rebirth of Otto's. Some people even mouthed the words to the song as she sang and strummed, filling her with some sorely needed confidence. A salve to her blistered wound of an ego.

Smiling to herself she ended the song and Damian's eyes slammed into hers almost like he thought the words she sang were for him when they clearly were not. Like they made him angry, which he shouldn't be because, again, the song was just a stupid song and had nothing to do with them. Had nothing to do with her running away from the best thing she'd ever been part of. Right? No. Not right. He knew the truth, the truth she kept trying to hide from herself. He knew every damn word was about him, about them.

But she didn't have time to debate with herself whether or not he was mad, or even why the hell he *was* mad because the entire crowd clapped, loudly. Well, nearly everyone except Carissa and her friends. Damian continued to stare at her, his face cranky, but he clapped...angrily, if that were possible.

Behind the farthest table, Damian's father stood at the long wooden bar that spanned the whole width of the room, talking with Colin. Well, more like aggressively talking *at* Colin. Whatever, there wasn't anything Jonathan Sloane could do to her that he hadn't already done. She'd sing and ignore him. Hell, she hadn't even realized he'd been there in the first place.

If only it were as easy to ignore the burn of Damian's gaze. If only she could close her eyes and he'd disappear along with this hollow ache that seemed to run along her seams, threatening to bust her wide open. Although, truth be told, whenever she closed her eyes he was all she'd see. But this Damian, the one glaring holes in her heart, was so different than the one she'd run from years before. This Damian smiled less, keeping his full mouth in a grim line. When he had smiled earlier that day it had been done either reluctantly, a simple curl at the edge of his beautiful lips, or cruelly, a hard line slashed across his face...a smile that didn't reach his eyes.

So she sang because that was just about all she had left. This time her words, her song...one she'd written when she'd been barely a teenager. She strangled the sobs that threatened to boil up from her belly when she thought about her situation, when she caught Damian's glare. She'd forged her path years ago and it was time to pay the piper. Her family was gone along with any remaining tie to the town. Her career had not only exploded but it had done so on a national scale. And the one man she'd ever loved was sitting at the bar watching her sing with a look she couldn't decipher. When heat—whether from the constant anger he wore proudly on his sleeve or from the constant sexual tension between them—flickered across his face in the shadowy light of the room she closed her eyes.

And she sang. When she finally opened her eyes Damian's spot at the bar was empty.

IT TOOK DAMIAN all of two songs before he had to step out into the cool night air to breathe. From the moment Kendall had opened her gorgeous mouth and sung her first word up there on that stage, it was like the air had been sucked from his lungs, from the room.

The ache in his estranged wife's voice still echoed through his body, ricocheting through his chest where his heart used to be and bouncing off his ribcage. From the initial licks of the guitar and first lyrics that shot at him like bullets from her mouth. He'd known she'd throw him off...her music always made him feel a little sideways. That had been a given. A foregone conclusion. What had been the real surprise was the visceral reaction to her standing up there with her eyes closed. He'd forgotten how much the music meant to her and just how much a part of her it was. It's why he'd walked out of that hall the one time he'd followed her to LA. He hadn't had the heart to try and take it away from her.

The door to the restaurant swung open with a whoosh as Damian pushed himself off the wall. Somehow he had to move beyond the hurricane of emotions swirling around in his head and move the fuck on. Only problem was he didn't quite know what moving on meant anymore. Did it mean paying off Kendall and seeing her on her way? Or did it mean convincing Kendall to stay and save their marriage?

"It wasn't bad enough she came back into town. You just had to rub our noses in it, didn't you?" His father walked toward him wearing a suit, as usual, and his usual scowl.

The way Damian was standing, angry and pissed, struck him like a punch to the jaw. Christ, he was turning into his father despite all his attempts to be just the opposite. But it was there, plain as the glare in his eyes, that Damian was on that same path. Constant dissatisfaction with life and circumstances. That was the crux of his father. Never happy no matter what he had. Never enough.

"Did she finally run home to tell on your big mean daddy?" His father stopped in front of him. "That girl never did have any sense."

"Don't be an ass. Her grandmother died. Don't pretend like you didn't know." Damian stepped forward, closing the distance between them, noting how much smaller his dad seemed now. When was the last time they'd had a real conversation? Probably never since a conversation with Jonathan Sloane always meant he was talking and the other participant was listening. His dad liked to educate and lecture. He wasn't much for listening. "And Kendall is still my wife."

His father snorted. His disdain was almost a real thing, another entity in the conversation. "She was never your wife. I could have her pulled off that stage and run her back out of town." Damian had never understood more than superficially his family's dislike for Kendall. Where she came from and who her family was wasn't something she could control any more than he could. His father disliked Kendall for no real reason, simply that she was not good enough for a Sloane, for Damian. His father had resented Damian and Kendall's instantaneous connection and the power it took away from him.

"No. You can't. And I won't let you. And neither will all those people in there listening to her sing. And she has always been my wife, Dad." Because he realized then that he had never not been in love with Kendall Kelly. He just hadn't allowed himself to think about it deeply in so long. At least not to the extent that he felt at that moment, deep in his bones.

A group of several people hustled up to the door and went in, filtering Kendall's sweet husky voice out. What the hell was he doing out here arguing with his dad? He may as well slam his head into the wall over and over for all the good it did him. His dad didn't listen and he wasn't interested in trying anyhow.

Kendall would be leaving soon enough, unless they discussed an alternative scenario, which was ridiculous because she had a career to get back to and a town to ditch. And he still didn't want to be the one who kept her from her dreams.

But what if she didn't? What if she stayed? What if he was her dream just as she was his?

But if she did stay, could he trust her again or would he always be waiting for her to leave in the middle of the night? And could she ever be happy in Blackberry Cove, the town she blamed for just about every wrong done to her?

"There's still a chance for you, son. Sell me the property—I can get you a great deal on it. You're still young enough to go back to school and do something with your life," his dad said, affecting a parental, and less aggressive stance. Well, at least, the truth was out there finally. His dad had always wanted that land.

"I heard about the resort developer's offer. Hell, they came directly to me the first time around. I'm not selling, so you can drop the 'good ole dad' routine. We both know you're full of shit," Damian said and watched as his father's face tightened and his eyes narrowed.

"Your mother was wrong about you. You're not special. You're nothing. Just another dirt farmer in a town of dirt farmers. At least your brother went and did something with his life. At least he's a hero."

"You're right about that. Duncan is a hero. But he joined the Army to get as far away from you as possible. You're also right about me, Dad. Not special at all." Damian placed his hand on the door and tugged, stopping for a moment before looking at his father over his shoulder. "And actually, I'm a goat farmer."

Kendall's voice hit him dead center in the chest, stopping him mid-step in the open doorway. She stood on that stage with her eyes closed, strumming her guitar to a rapt audience. She stood proud, her long ruffled sweater framing her lean body, her voice climbing. It grew and grew and washed over him like a wave, a wave meant to wash clean the sins of the past and his fear of the future. There was only now and there was only her.

He had absolutely no clue how to move forward but he was sick of being stuck in the past, sick of slowly turning into his bitter old man, and sick of allowing his woman to wander the world without knowing how he felt about her or that she had a home with him. That he'd wait for her. Hell, he'd even leave this place for her.

The thought shook him as he stepped back into Otto's and slid into the booth next to Delilah. She flashed him a wide smile that abruptly fell. "Are you okay?"

He nodded. And for the first time in four years he was okay. No matter what happened, he would be all right. Good even. And if he had his way, maybe Kendall would be too.

Chapter Eleven

KENDALL FINISHED HER short set to booming applause that filled all her empty spaces and made her feel whole. The roar of clapping hands and hoots from townspeople she thought despised her did weird things to her belly, making her feel wildly uncomfortable in her own skin, but strangely excited at the same time.

She loved performing. She always had. However, the past two years she had begun to hate the drama and large-scale productions that bordered on theatre her shows had become. That had been all Ben. Ben's additions to her shows had been so subtle at first—a new backup singer here, a lower cut costume there, an extra night here—that she'd barely noticed. He'd been the experienced one of the crew, the one they deferred to on all things music business.

"Now, darlin', who's the star maker here?" he'd ask her with his weird little laugh. "Let me do my job." So she had. Even though her gut had told her to get a better handle on her career, Ben had assured her she was the talent and he was the businessman. She'd approved his changes until he stopped asking and just made them on his own without her input. She'd accepted his explanations every time lies were printed about her or pictures were leaked of her with a new guy. He said that all PR was good and that her heartbreaker image would sell records and concert tickets. It didn't matter that the photos were all contrived and that she went out less and less. Soon her life outside of her small LA apartment consisted of only concerts, media appearances, and practice.

Ben had even forged her signature on the contract for the last recording offer saying she gave her approval "by proxy." By the time he'd disappeared with her advance, her band had unraveled and quit—apparently, they preferred to be paid actual money instead of promises for services rendered—and she'd lost her taste for the business of music. She couldn't write, couldn't sing, couldn't even listen to any kind of music without a gaping yaw of grief and emptiness. Unfortunately, the record company could care less about her feelings. They either wanted a record or they wanted their cash back. After her repeated excuses for canceled shows and postponing practices, they just wanted their money back.

Until the call from her former producer. Now the label was interested in making a deal. Maybe they'd gotten calls from fans, maybe from venue owners or sponsors. She didn't really know. Frankly, didn't really care. She was willing to do anything they wanted if it meant getting straight with them, wasn't she? Whether it was cut the album or go back on the road, that's what she'd do. Then Damian could keep his profits and run the farm the way he wanted to. And she wouldn't have to take any more from the man who'd tried to give her everything.

And now she was back in Blackberry Cove and she'd found her voice again. Her eyes flew to the man sitting with Delilah. God, he was beautiful. Sitting there in his cowboy shirt with the pearled snaps and those perfectly cut jeans. All man, focused on her with a huge grin that transformed his handsome face into something from the gods. How had she ever walked away from him? How had she been so deluded to think there could ever be anything or anyone that remotely compared to him let alone replace him altogether?

But fear was a powerful motivator and she was driven by it. Something sharp tightened in her chest. Was her fear stronger than Damian? This time around would she be brave enough to do what was right instead of letting her emotions, her fear, dictate her direction?

As she made her way back to the booth, she was greeted by well-wishers—among them old classmates, a former teacher, new residents, the minister and his wife. Never in her entire time in Blackberry Cove had she been so accepted, felt so much a part of the town. She wondered if maybe she had been a little bit too severe in her condemnation of the entire town because...because of her damn fear.

But before she could go deeper with that thought she was standing in front of Damian and Delilah. Damian stood, unfurling his long body from his seat, and stood toe to toe with her so that she had to bend her neck up to see his face, that handsome face with the big smile. "Hello, wife," he said simply, all traces of the enigmatic anger from earlier gone.

"Hello, husband," she said quietly, not wanting to break the spell he'd cast.

Reaching for her hand with his, he bent down and kissed her full on the mouth. Another public claiming, another proclamation that she didn't quite know the meaning of. He pulled back slightly; at the same time he drew his arm tighter around her waist, his lips barely touching hers. "That was amazing, sweetheart. I've never seen you look more beautiful."

Her forehead was damp from performing, but her skin caught fire and warmth crept up her neck and down her torso. This man did her in. Broke her open and left her feeling exposed. Every. Damn. Time. Her heart grew, pushing against her ribs, making it hard to breathe. He pulled back and brushed his lips over her cheek and whispered into her ear. "I'll be over at the bar having a beer. You finish your visit with Delilah. And then I'm taking you home to remind you why we're so good together."

The hot lick of flames building in her body was mirrored in his eyes, but there was something else there too. Was there a little bit of a threat crouched there in his gaze or in the possessive hold on her hand. What did he mean? Sex...he must be talking about sex. They were always great that way—their chemistry was undeniable even now. Her heart deflated. At least they would always have that. She would take what she could get and be happy with it since she'd given it all up so long ago. She'd just have to ignore the weird settling-in feeling she had whenever he held her, but it was getting just as hard to ignore as the erection pressing into her hip.

Swallowing hard she wrapped her arms around his waist and squeezed, allowing herself a moment to lay her head on his hard chest, letting his warmth and strength seep into her skin, into her bones. This *would* be enough. It would have to be.

Kendall kissed his shirt right where it covered his heart and then slid into the booth. "I'll just have one drink and then we can go, okay?"

"Yep." He turned and nodded to Delilah. "It was good to see you again, D. Don't be a stranger." And then he disappeared into the crowd.

"He's different. The same, but different," Delilah said.

Kendall ordered an iced tea and turned back to her friend. "Yeah. Tender and thoughtful still, but rougher and more aggressive. More...I don't know..."

"Possessive," Delilah offered with a teasing lilt.

Kendall nodded. "The boy I married grew into a man while I was gone."

"A pretty angry man. But not so much right now." Delilah narrowed her eyes at Kendall. "Be careful. If you leave him again he's liable to snap altogether."

Kendall sighed, a deep, dramatic breath in and out.

Wasn't that the truth? And she couldn't bear to hurt him like that again, but she had to go make it right with the label. And making it right with them might very well mean she'd have to record an album she didn't have any interest in making and then touring to support it. Either that or she'd end up taking Damian's money and giving it to the label, but then Damian would probably still want her to go.

"I know. But…" She paused. How much to tell Delilah? Maybe she should just trust her friend for once. Kendall took a sip from her tea, looked her friend in the eye with her most sincere expression. What she saw on Delilah's face wasn't really a surprise, an answering tacit assurance that she could trust her…that she'd always been able to trust her. Starting from the beginning when both her father-in-law and her grandmother had confronted her and ending with the call from her rep at the label, she spilled all her secrets, ending with the odd exchange with Damian's mom and her sprained-not-sprained ankle.

"I almost think she insisted I go for an X-ray so she could spend time with us."

"Us?"

"Yeah. Both of us. His mom seemed genuinely heartbroken about the crumbling relationship with her son and totally remorseful about her part in pushing me away. She hinted at leaving Mr. Sloane. It was all kind of surreal."

"Maybe she is sorry. I mean, she's his mother. Both her sons aren't part of her life anymore and her husband is a controlling asshole who doesn't have a nice thing to say about anyone. You know, kind of like your grandmother," Delilah said and it was a shock to Kendall. Because it was so true. Her grandma and his father were very much the same despite the details of their lives. They consistently chose misery over love or happiness to make themselves feel more important, more powerful, more relevant. Maybe that's why her grandmother had told her about her mother in the manner she had. Maybe it wasn't really true. Or, if it was, maybe it didn't matter because love was so much stronger than misery, or fear.

Kendall looked around the room, observing the crowd, but always searching for that one face. Damian's. He was there at the end of the bar, sipping a bottle of beer and talking with Brian and Colin. He smiled at her, the curve of his mouth hidden behind his bottle, but she could see it in his eyes even across the room. The soft crinkle of his eyes and the dip of his head told her everything. He was watching her just like she was looking for him.

Colin clipped him on the shoulder and Damian turned back to the conversation. Remembering Delilah's bristly reaction to Colin she asked, "What's the deal with you and Colin?"

"No deal," Delilah said. Kendall waited for her to fill in the empty spaces but Delilah just sipped her water and said nothing.

"Liar. I told you everything. Now it's your turn."

"First nothing happened. He asked me out and then flaked on me. Not once, but twice. I never give a guy a third chance. But he doesn't seem to want to give up. End of story."

Kendall decided that there was definitely more to that story and it sounded infinitely better than discussing her kerfuffle of a life at that moment.

"You're not going to tell me anything else, are you?" Kendall asked. But Delilah clearly wouldn't be persuaded to disclose more and seemed dead set on helping Kendall unscrew her own issues.

"Nope. But I will tell you one thing. Love, real love, like you and Damian have had since you were a teenager is a rare and beautiful thing, my friend. And if I were you I'd consider that before you make your next move. Speaking of which, punk rock cowgirl, what's your plan? How do you appease the suits at your label, pay back the money that douchebag stole from you, and keep your husband?"

Kendall shrugged. "Here's the thing. If I leave again he'll never trust me to come back. Would you?" Of course Delilah wouldn't. Hell, she wouldn't even give a hot guy a third chance at a date. "Yeah. Didn't think so."

"Have you told him about the call?"

"Nope. And I don't want to keep it from him. I really do want to tell him everything. I'm just afraid that it will be the end of us for good." Because she'd already hurt him so badly, she was terrified he'd never trust her to come back, never trust her not to just stay gone. What if that look that was coming back in his eyes went away? That terrified her more than anything.

"SWEETHEART, WE'RE HOME." Damian unbuckled his sleeping wife's seat belt and pulled her into his arms. Her hands automatically wound around his neck as he lifted her and kicked the truck door closed with his foot.

"Cold," she mumbled, burrowing against his chest a little, and sighed. "What time is it?"

"Nearly midnight." They'd dropped Delilah off at her little rental house in town before driving home to the farm. Home. Was this their home now or was he living in a fantasy, the one he'd tried for so long to erase from his mind? He walked through the darkened house straight to the bedroom and set her gently on his bed.

Kendall struggled to sit up, but he placed his hand on her shoulder and pushed her back on the bed before sitting next to her. The bed shifted, and her body rolled into his slightly. Pulling one booted foot onto his thigh he ran his hands from her delicate ankle up her calf, slowly massaging the soft flesh underneath the suede. Her low moan as he reached her thigh and pulled the tab on the boot zipper, easing it down slowly, filled him with so much masculine pride. God, he loved this woman.

Damian's hands froze on her leg.

He loved Kendall.

No. No he didn't.

But he did. And he probably always had, never stopped. Yes, he'd been angry and felt hollowed out like a rotting tree, still alive, but just barely. But that had never kept him from loving her or missing her or wanting her back.

He kept moving the zipper down and the rich female scent of arousal reached his nose and he inhaled sharply, filling his lungs with her as if trying to replace the stagnant air he'd been breathing for years. His desire for her was overwhelming, an entire body experience, even though she was clearly hiding something from him. She'd stepped away from him that afternoon to take a call she seemed none too pleased to receive. Afterward she'd been distant, obviously working over something in her head. He knew she wanted to share it with him, and yet she hadn't. And just as he'd begun to feel anger and revert to his distrust of her he was struck by a thought. Perhaps he'd never really demonstrated his trust of her. Not really.

Maybe he'd been so caught up in keeping her, tethering Kendall to him, the farm, and Blackberry Cove, that he'd only pretended at trust. Only pretended at marriage and being a family. He'd always laid the burden of not under-standing family at his wife's feet, but since he hadn't come from the most loving of family environments perhaps he was just as much to blame.

So maybe it was time to give her the benefit of the doubt for once and trust her to sort out whatever that call was about. And since it probably had more to do with her life away from him than her life with him, he shouldn't push her so much. If Kendall was meant to be with him then she would be. If she wasn't, well they'd cross that burning bridge when they got to it.

Damian tugged off her boot and set it beside the bed before moving to her other leg, placing her boot on his thigh. This time he considered her eyes as he worked his way up her leg. "You're still the most beautiful woman I've ever seen."

She smiled but it didn't reach her eyes. "You sound surprised." Her voice was low, gravelly like it always was after she performed, with a breathless edge that was pretty much the sexiest thing he'd ever heard.

"I suppose I shouldn't be. I was just so pissed for so long. I guess I forgot."

"About how I look?" She lazily quirked a brow.

"No, baby, about how you make me feel." He pulled her other boot off and set it next to the one on the floor.

"You don't feel angry?"

"Anger is definitely not what I'm feeling right now." He smirked. He needed to get the rest of her clothes off. Like now.

"I think these pants are going to be more of a challenge. I basically painted them on." Her hands flew to the buttons on the front of her leather pants, but he brushed them away.

"Oh no, sweetheart, that's my job. I haven't thought about anything else since I saw you walk into the room with those pants on earlier tonight."

Slowly he peeled her pants off, admiring the reveal of pale skin beneath the dark leather. He made quicker work of her T-shirt and bra before sitting back on his heels and admiring her body laid out on his bed, a veritable buffet of sex, of beauty so deep it made his heart beat harder. She gave him a sweet smile and it woke something hot, something possessive and needy inside him.

The absolute conviction that she belonged with him here in Blackberry Cove rolled over him like a semi-truck. He wasn't sure how much longer he'd be able to push these feelings back. There were so many truths, both spoken and not, that needed to be aired. But for now he would concentrate on her body. For now he would focus on her and this thing building between them. The decision of whether or not he was up for the battle for her heart would have to wait.

"Put your hands above your head." He practically growled at her, but she didn't flinch, just moved her hands above her head in an elegant, fluid movement. So sweet. So beautiful. So ready for him and only him. Was he an asshole because he knew he was the only man to touch Kendall? Probably. He didn't care. Not one bit. She was his and she always had been.

"Grab on to the headboard," he ordered and pulled protection from the drawer and tossed it on the bed. Kendall bit into her bottom lip and wrapped her fingers around the iron bars of the headboard.

He undressed quickly and sheathed himself, keeping his eyes pinned to hers, loving the way her chest rose and fell on shallow breaths, the way her fingers gripped the headboard so tightly they were turning white, the way he knew she wanted him. And he just didn't have it in him to question what he was doing, how far down this path he was willing to go before she turned right while he went left.

When Damian crawled over her and settled in between her thighs, he took her mouth with his, showing her with his body what he couldn't tell her. Not yet. Then he stroked his hands down her curves and explored her as if he hadn't memorized every rounded peak years ago. He stroked and licked and sucked and bit until she was nearly sobbing for release.

"Come for me, baby," he said and plunged his fingers into her and rubbed that tight bundle of nerves. Kendall cried out his name and her whole body went rigid.

Before her breathing normalized he removed her hands from the iron slats and placed them on his shoulders, then slid one hand under her and lifted her. Finally he slid his achingly hard cock into her pliant body and then everything else simply faded away.

And it wasn't until she was wrapped in his arms later that night that he realized she still hadn't told him about the call.

Chapter Twelve

DAMIAN LAY IN bed thinking about how Kendall had got up on that stage and sung her heart out that night despite the glares and overly loud whispered comments. The old Kendall, the one Damian had fallen in love with and married, would have crawled up into his lap and cried. Or just plain run away. She'd spent the whole of her time in town running from bullies, including her own grandmother. This Kendall was different. This Kendall stood up to her hecklers that night and got up on that stage with her head held high before belting out songs that had everyone jumping to their feet in appreciation.

For some reason that felt like someone had ripped out his dusty old heart and replaced it with another one. His old one.

Damian wasn't sure yet if he liked it. In fact, he was pretty sure he didn't. And when she looked at him with her eyes wide and her lips parted in expectation it made his old heart beat a little too hard and feel a little too big in his chest.

"I need to tell you something, Damian," she said quietly, running her slender fingers over his chest. Back and forth in a soothing, almost hypnotic pattern. "Actually I need to tell you a couple things."

He pulled himself up and settled against the headboard, pretending his newly revived heart hadn't dropped down into his stomach.

"The first thing is that no matter what happens moving forward, I need you to know how much this time together has meant to me." She took a deep breath. "I know you think my decision to leave was wrong. And maybe you're right. Maybe I should have fought back and not been such a coward." She pressed her fingers to his lips when he started to interrupt her. "No let me finish."

He had to tell her what she meant to him. That he thought he'd forgiven her. Or he could. Maybe he had. But she had more she wanted to say and he had to let her.

"I never stopped thinking about you, Damian. Never stopped loving you. I honestly thought I was doing the right thing. I swear I did. I know you don't agree, but do you at least understand what I tried to do?"

He nodded, despite the reservations he still had about moving forward, and nipped at her fingertips. He was beginning to believe that maybe she'd needed to leave, needed to be out on her own in order to realize what she had at home.

"Stop it," she said with such a stern look on her face.

"But you're so sexy when you're all contrite and stuff." He kissed her nose.

"Shut up and let me finish." She smiled but didn't laugh. "It's okay if you don't feel like I do. But I love you. I've never not loved you."

His stomach clenched and his breath stopped for a beat. He hadn't expected this: that she would just come out and say the words that seemed stuck in his chest. But there was something else, something she hadn't said, and it hung in the air like ash after a firestorm.

"But..." And there it was. She shifted and her hand stopped moving on his chest. *Move your damn hand, Kendall. Don't stop...just don't stop.*

"Does this have anything to do with that call?" he prompted. *Just get it over with, darlin'. One swing of the axe and we'll be done.*

She nodded. "The rep from my label called. They know what Ben did and they want me to come to LA and discuss my options." Her smile was weak, and her eyes were shiny but she held her chin high and held his gaze.

"And what does that mean?" He could feel her already moving away from him. The distance was growing and there wasn't a damn thing he could do about it. She didn't say anything, just stared at him and swallowed. "You have to leave? Again?"

Kendall bit her lip, closed her eyes, and leaned back on the headboard. "Yes."

That clenching in his stomach changed, shifted, spread through his body until he could barely breathe. "What are your options?" he asked, a little hope still fighting for air in the room. What if she wanted to stay? What if he could get her to? Of course, maybe she didn't want to. She'd always hated this town and had never felt part of it. Fuck. What kind of man would ask the woman he loved to stay in a place she despised? What kind of man would keep the woman he loved from pursuing her dreams?

Not him. Not this time. He took a deep breath and resolved to let her go. If that's what she really wanted, he would love her enough to let her go. The idea of her leaving him again, this time for good, made his heart hurt along with his gut. But he would do it. For her.

"They want to talk in person so I don't know yet what their angle is, but there's no way to get around the money I owe them. It's not the label's fault Ben took the money. It's mine."

"Have they considered going after him legally?"

She shrugged one naked, pale shoulder. "They gave the advance to me. I gave it to him to manage. I'm the one at fault." She had a point. Unfortunately. "There are only a couple ways this can go. They want the money back immediately. Or they make me work for it."

"What does that look like it? Working for it, I mean."

A bleak, sad look fluttered across her face making him want to reach out and cradle her head in his hands. But they had to get through this conversation first. Then they could talk about the future. However that looked.

"I make another record and then go back on the road to support it. Money is made on the road now. Merch and tickets."

"What do you want to do?" *Stay here with me. Where you belong.* How could it feel so right for her to be here if this wasn't where she was supposed to be?

"I want to go back in time and never have left you, if I'm being honest." Her voice was quiet, but there was steel behind her fragility. She was trying to right her wrongs—he could see that. And she was doing it bravely. "And I want to talk to your mom about what my grandmother said about my mom."

"Well, I'm going to vote for honesty right now. I told you I'd buy you out. You can pay them back and then decide what you want to do."

"I don't want your money anymore. Now that I know what you could do with this farm and that money. I've already taken enough," she bit out, like the words cut coming out her mouth.

"So you want to leave? Go back on the road?"

"No, Damian, I don't." She shifted on the bed, pulling the sheet tight across her chest.

"But you don't want to stay here either."

"I don't know what I want. Tonight. The last couple weeks. I'm so confused."

The anger and tension he'd been holding back with sheer will floated to the top. Hell, it swam to the top with the ferocity of a great white shark. And it wanted blood. He was tired of these back and forth games with her. Tired of not knowing how she felt or if she'd ever want to stay. Of course she'd go back on the road if the opportunity presented itself. What a classic fool he was.

"Once again, you're leaving. When?"

"Damian…" Her tone turned placating and her face paled.

"When, Kendall?" he demanded, his anger growing along with his need to escape this conversation and its inevitable conclusion.

"Tomorrow morning. Ten." Her answer couldn't have surprised him more if she'd delivered it with a slap. She was leaving in the morning, just a few short hours from now.

"How long?"

"I don't know. A week?"

"You planning on coming back?"

"I want to…" And there was his answer in the words she didn't say. She wanted to but she just didn't know how she could do both: be the punk rock cowgirl and the farmer's wife.

"What the fuck does that mean, Kendall? Are you coming back or not? I need to know this time. Because I'm not pining after you anymore. I want to get on with my life."

"With me or without me?" she asked, her face waxen.

"Well, I guess that depends on you, sweetheart. Doesn't it?"

"Does it, Damian? Or are you already pushing me away because you're afraid of loving me again?" Yeah, he probably was. But maybe this time he wanted to head the pain off at the pass and perhaps dole out a little of his own. He was sick of being the only casualty of this marriage.

"I'm not afraid of loving you, Kendall. I'm afraid of betting on the wrong horse."

Clearly he'd said the worst of all the horrible things since her face turned a dark shade of red and she jumped from the bed and moved straight into the closet. He wanted to go to her and soothe her with his body, with the words he couldn't quite get out. And he wanted her to feel just a tiny a bit of the pain he'd carried around for years. So he didn't go to her. He stayed on the bed, frozen. By anger. By betrayal. By an age-old bitterness that he couldn't quite let go of.

When she emerged from the closet she was wearing yoga pants that he shouldn't notice molded to her curves, and a gray hoodie. His gray hoodie. God, he loved when she wore his clothes. He should tell her that. Tell her how he really felt, but the words just wouldn't form on his tongue.

She stared at him for a moment, not moving. Then asked, "Do you love me, Damian?"

All he could manage was a terse, "Where are you going?" And terror and ache and want and everything he'd been holding back with his stupid walls broke free and flooded his chest. But he still couldn't say it. Couldn't tell her the truth. She was finally being honest and he couldn't get past his own fear.

"Fuck you, Damian Sloane. You are a coward and we both deserve better." Was the last thing he heard as he stood naked in front of his living room window watching the love of his life stomp across his yard and onto the back porch of her grandmother's house.

KENDALL FOUND HERSELF up the next morning before the sun even dared peek its angry head over the hills surrounding the valley Kelly Family Farms rested in. She had packed the night before and since she'd turned in her rental car the week before, the shuttle she'd scheduled the previous afternoon rolled up right on time and just before Damian would be up to let the goats out and start his work day.

And though she never looked back as the small minivan pulled down the driveway and out onto the main road she could feel him watching as she left. Her eyes burned from the endless tears she'd shed during the night, but they were thankfully dry now. She was grateful, at least, for that.

"Up kind of early, aren't you, ma'am?" said the driver as he glanced at her in the rearview mirror. He had kind eyes. But then again her judgment of character had been sucky at best. For all she knew he could be a serial killer.

"Yep. Early flight."

The man nodded and looked forward, taking the hint

that she was not feeling chatty. Kendall stared out the window at the gorgeous landscape of Blackberry Cove unfurling against the stunning colors of dawn. Normally this was when she'd be happy to be leaving the dirt patch that had been nothing but misery for her.

But everything had changed, turned upside down. She hadn't really hated Blackberry Cove, had she? She'd been unloved by her family and Damian's family sure, but had the town really been so awful? She had favorite teachers and a best friend and she'd had Damian. But that hadn't been enough for her, had it? She'd demanded more and more and more until no one had anything left to give.

So she'd left. Take that, everyone! And thumbed her nose on her way out. Then played the martyr for four years. Hating her life on the road, the demands of music people, the fans, the late nights, and parties. She'd been over-whelmed from the beginning, longing for some semblance of quiet and routine. The erratic demands of tour life and the unpredictable hours were brutal. She'd lamented the loss of her love, playing the tragic heroine in her own ridiculous tragedy.

But she hadn't given anyone, least of all her husband, the opportunity to fight for her. For them. Instead she'd blamed them all for her life, but never taken responsibility. Running, running, running.

The realization struck her like a thunderbolt. Blackberry Cove was home. Was where she belonged all along. Or maybe not. Maybe she'd needed to take this road to discover it led directly back to where she'd started. Kelly Family Farms. But it was all too late, wasn't it? She'd finally come clean and admitted everything, but he hadn't done the same. He'd been frozen there with that stricken look on his face like he was about to say it, like he wanted to. But he hadn't and that had said more than anything.

This time though she wasn't running. She was fixing her mess and then she was going to make him see they really were meant to be together.

No matter what happened with the label executives she would call Damian afterward and discuss their requests. She would tell him she loved him yet again and that she trusted him and that she wanted nothing more than to be back on the farm...farming. Being his wife. Playing with her goats, loving that big dog and that mean old donkey. If he could accept her the way she was, she would stop running. Stop pretending she was something she wasn't. Even if it meant starting over and dating her own husband. Because she needed him. Loved him. And intended to try and keep him.

Forever.

"We're here," the driver said as he pulled up to the one terminal. She handed him some cash and he got out to grab her bags. "Whatever put that sadness in your eyes, I hope it gets better."

"Thank you. I hope so too. I'm going to do everything I can to make sure it does." She smiled at him and went to check in.

Her flight went quickly and she thought it a good sign they'd booked her for first class, even though the small plane didn't actually boast first class service. They'd also reserved a lovely hotel room for her just outside of Hollywood for an indefinite span of time, which was helpful since she'd given up her apartment in West Hollywood and shoved what few belongings she'd had into a small storage unit before making her way to Blackberry Cove.

After checking in to her hotel room, she threw herself on the bed. And stared at her phone for a good ten minutes before clicking on Damian's name in her contacts. He would be out working and wouldn't hear his phone even if the call actually went through—hard to know if it would with their dodgy service out on the farm. It rang five times before she heard his voice message. Her heart stopped for a moment and her chest hurt. How could his recorded voice have such an impact on her?

Damian Sloane of Kelly Family Farms. You know what to do.

"Damian, it's me. I just wanted to say I'm sorry. I love you and I want us to work this out. I already miss you. Please call me as soon as you can," but before hanging up she paused and then added, "I wish you were here."

Well if that wasn't being honest and spelling it out, Kendall didn't know what was. And now it was recorded. No going back from *I love you and I want us to work this out.*

There was only going forward. With this meeting. With her career. But most importantly with her life and with Damian. If she had to cut another album and go on the road, she would. She was done being spoiled. She would be glad for the opportunity to repay her debt and create some art while she was doing it. She would be glad for the chance to go home, eventually, to the man she loved. And hopefully he still loved her, though he hadn't said the words yet.

No matter, she thought as she pulled on a black pantsuit and topped it off with a pair of black rhinestones boots, she was taking responsibility for her life and her love.

The ride to the label offices was quick and didn't give her much time to balk at her new resolve or talk herself out of it. Almost too swiftly she was ushered into a conference room with her rep, two other men, and a woman in casual but expensive clothing. Conversation stopped and they all stood when she entered and each one introduced themselves before sitting.

The woman was the head of sponsorship. The older man was her rep's boss and the other man the deputy head of the country division. All bigwigs, which she found interesting. Did that mean they were here to intimidate her into repaying the advance or convince her to go back on the road? It was hard tell from their enigmatic looks which direction the meeting was going to take.

Since Ben had acted as her agent from the beginning of her career when he'd found her singing in a small restaurant after hours to a crowd of approximately three people, she'd never actually sat at the conference table without representation, without someone who had a vested interest in her career, and her resolve flagged slightly. Who was she to think she could go up against the management of her label and win?

Nobody. That's who she was. Just a poor little unwanted orphan from a pothole in middle of California. She took a deep breath to fortify herself, shore up her flagging supports, and said, "What's the agenda for this meeting? I feel like I'm the only one here without a directive?" She laughed a deep chuckle, going for warm and mature, not self-deprecating.

Her faux confidence seemed to do the trick and the tension in the room thinned.

Mary Wells, the head of sponsorship, spoke first. "We want to say how happy we are to have you with Reckless Media. It's unfortunate that we've come to this point and even more so that you've had so many…issues with your management team." Kendall wasn't clear how much they had known coming into the meeting. They had canceled her record after she had said she didn't want to tour for at least twelve months and record for at least six. Strike while the iron is hot, they'd said. Building momentum is the key, they'd repeatedly told her, as her sales began to drop. But she'd been so weary. So exhausted from everything having to do with music. She'd just wanted out. So they'd agreed to take her advance back and let her out of the rest of her contract. But the money had been gone along with her business manager so she'd asked for more time.

And time had run out.

"Previously we agreed to release you from your contract in exchange for repayment of your advance. We've since learned it's unlikely you'll be able to do so because of your business manager," Mary continued with a grin that seemed neither warm, nor remotely genuine. In fact, it lent her classically pretty face a cold, almost wizened air. "We'd like to discuss your options and come to a resolution based on your input." What the hell did that even mean? *Based on her input* sounded like they would decide her future regardless of her *input*.

That wasn't happening. Maybe when she left Los Angeles nearly three weeks before she would have perhaps rolled over and let them see her belly almost immediately. But something had changed. Hell, who was she kidding? Everything had changed. However, before she went off or said something impulsive she only nodded, wordlessly requesting Mary continue with her spiel.

The meeting went on for over three painful hours. The label executives took turns praising her before they dug their nails into her skin. They ruthlessly provided a list of every bad review, every unsold-out show, every negative article on her fake relationships, and then the coup de grace of them all: her naive dependence on a known music business con man.

Near the end of the third hour, she politely cut into the latest diatribe from her rep, Morgan Bales. "Morgan, pardon me. While I appreciate all the background information, I was there. This is my career. I'm fully aware of what has or hasn't happened. And I know what needs to change, should I continue recording and touring. But what we haven't addressed is what exactly my options are." Morgan was clearly surprised by her words and opened his mouth to respond before the division head cleared his throat, effectively shutting down everyone else in the room.

The man in charge of the country music division, Robert Smith, who had sat quietly and watched the discussions—ha, more like lectures, but okay—placed his elbows on the table and folded his hands in front of him, and then finally spoke. "Ms. Kelly, we're in the business of making music, but more importantly we're in the business of making stars, building lifelong careers for young entertainers like yourself." He paused for effect, Kendall was sure. Everything about the attractive older man was calculated and practiced. You didn't reach his level of success and stay there for two decades by being impulsive and friendly. But instead of letting him finish his little speech Kendall chuckled. Not on purpose, truth be told. She'd behaved and played by their rules for hours, but their pomposity and carefully disguised condescension had about reached the limit on her bullshit meter.

Besides the wide-eyed surprise on Smith's face was worth all of it. Heck even if she had to go back on the road as essentially a modern-day indentured servant, it would be worth it. And, really, she wasn't childish enough to believe that being a music star and having fans was anything less than amazing. She would deal with the anxiety and pressure. She would make the best of it by making good music and sharing it with the world. And when she was done she could go back home and fight for her marriage and her place on their farm.

Because that's what the farm and Blackberry Cove were…they were home. And Damian—he was the center of it. She missed him so much, and for a moment she was struck by just how very much she wished he were there by her side. His tall strong body sitting beside her right then would go a long way toward shoring up her flagging confidence. And loneliness.

"Reckless is in business to make money. Don't get me wrong, I'm grateful I got to be part of that for a while. But I'm a product. I know that. The way I see it is that I have one of two options. Option one I pay you the money I owe for the advance and you let me out of my contract. The other option is I record another album and go on tour to support it therefore providing me the opportunity to earn the advance back." She looked around the table at a group of faces that were seconds away from calling her new tough-guy bluff and demanding the money before showing her to the door.

"At this point, Ms. Kelly, we'd prefer you to record another album and then support it."

"I appreciate your honesty. However, that means I go on the road and do interviews and media spots."

"Correct."

"What if I would prefer to not do that and just pay back the advance and call it a day?" she asked noticing they had omitted that possibility.

"That's no longer an option," Mr. Smith said, attempting to close the door on her walking away.

Her hands grew clammy in her lap and she resisted the almost overwhelming urge to rub them on her clothes. Instead she kept her fingers flat on her legs, even keeping herself from tapping her finger on her wrist. Fidgeting would be tantamount to showing her fear and then they'd go in for the kill.

"It is though. I have the amendment to my contract in writing, therefore it remains an option." She could tell they hadn't expected her to fight back or, at least, explore all the possibilities when they all stared at their notebooks and flipped pages. Their assumption had been that she'd gratefully do what they requested. That was the behavior her rep had seen from her time and time again. And, of course, it probably didn't matter because she didn't have the money, but she did want to know what was possible going forward.

"We're prepared to offer you extended points for recording and touring in addition to clearing your advance." And they showed their hand right then and there. They wanted her on the road. They wanted new music from her.

"That's very generous, however, I'm not quite sure I want to go back on the road." That had been fine before, but now they looked apoplectic as if she'd turned down a ten-carat diamond engagement ring. "I'd like to take the rest of the day to think about it. Can we reconvene tomorrow morning?"

"Of course. Although can you give us a feel for what you're thinking and your direction moving forward?" Mr. Smith asked.

"No, I can't." And that was the truth. Kendall Kelly knew what she wanted, but had no idea what she was going to do or how to get it. She suspected what she really wanted was too far out of reach and wasn't hers to claim any longer and that thought had her ending the meeting and running for the bathroom where she promptly dry heaved the sandwich they'd had brought in for lunch.

Chapter Thirteen

D AMIAN HEARD THE car pull up and the door slam before his mother's voice called from the open door of his office.

"Damian Sloane, what the hell are you doing here?" Well, he hadn't expected to see her so soon again. Although he did still need to make plans to meet for dinner. Damian was serious about trying to repair his severely degraded relationship with his mother.

Damian looked up from signing the last check of the week, glad to have the bills done. "Hello to you too, Mom. Please, why don't you come in?" He motioned to the only other chair in the room. He hid his smile when his normally calm mother stomped into the dusty farm office and stood in front of his desk glaring down at him.

"Is there something I can help you with?" he asked, folding his checkbook and placing it into his backpack on the floor. "Or are you here to reschedule our dinner?"

"Why are you still here and not with Kendall in Los Angeles?" she asked ignoring his question and sighing dramatically before flopping into the old chair. For the first time since she'd walked in he realized she wasn't nearly as perfectly put together as Dr. Sloane usually was. Her hair was pulled back in a haphazard ponytail and she was wearing some kind of lounging workout suit.

"Mom, what's going on?" He pushed his chair back from the desk and kicked his legs out, crossing them at the ankles. "How did you know Kendall was in Los Angeles?"

"She called me about an hour ago." Nothing his mother could have said would have surprised him more. "Also, I left your father." Except perhaps that.

"Whoa. Okay. Let's start with leaving Dad. What happened?" Because that was easier than talking about Kendall. The searing pain of her walking out on him early this morning still sat hot and jagged in his chest. The look on her face when she called him a coward frozen into his brain.

"Let's not start there. Let's start with your marriage, which is salvable—unlike mine, which isn't."

"Fine."

"Yes, fine. Here's the thing, son, I've made so many mistakes, too many to count or recall so I'm here now to tell you: do not be like me. And certainly don't be like your father. Be you, Damian, be the man who knows what's right and what he wants. And then go get it. Go get her. She needs you there. She needs someone to run after her for once and bring her home."

"I wasn't so sure, Mom. I was too afraid to let her back in and now she's gone."

"She said she left you a message." His mom's face lit with expectation. Despite her disheveled appearance, she seemed calm now, unlike her ambush moments ago when she'd barreled up to him.

He nodded and rubbed his hand over the back of his neck. "She did." He had listened to it as soon as he saw it, but the connection had been too garbled to understand it. Nevertheless he'd made flight arrangements and wrapped up his work so he could go be with her. "It was too hard to understand."

"But you're going?"

"Yes," he said simply. "What did she say to you?"

His mother sighed again, the kind of deep sigh that only a long-suffering mother can make. "She told me where she was. That she still had another meeting tomorrow at ten. And she wanted to know my medical opinion of the utter baloney her grandmother had told her."

Damian had completely forgotten about Kendall's fears that she might pass on some kind of mystery drug addiction illness to their children. But she hadn't forgotten. In fact, in her mind it was the justification she'd needed to give in to her fear and run.

"I told her that her grandmother was a cruel woman, much like my own husband, who took hostages instead of having relationships with other humans. That it was very unlikely that anything that woman ever told her was the truth. And that she should live her life and have a family."

He bowed his head and thanked the universe as relief flooded his body. Because it had never mattered to him, but it did to Kendall. "Thank you, Mom." Damian stood and moved toward his mother. Placing his hands around her upper arms he pulled her from her chair and wrapped her in his arms. "Thank you," he said again as his mother buried her head in his chest and he felt soft sobs wrack her body.

After a few minutes he kissed the top of her head and asked, "Did you kick Dad out?"

She shook her head. "I left. I couldn't justify his behavior anymore. I couldn't pretend I still loved him when I didn't. And I couldn't come to you and push you to follow your heart if I didn't do the same." She patted his arm and pulled back. "When do you leave?"

He'd already finished giving his staff their instructions for the next couple days, putting Coleman in charge of the farm and Samantha in charge of production and the shop. They were a well-oiled team that would work the farm and business seamlessly.

He glanced at the clock on the wall. "I should probably get out of here in a couple minutes. But first…" Damian pulled open the drawer of a filing cabinet and pulled out a metal box. He unlocked the box and dug around for something before presenting his mother with a key. "This is the key to the main house here. It's in a bit of disarray because we've been working on it, but you are welcome to stay there for now." Although if he had his way, he'd come home with his wife and make the old farmhouse their home, and his mom would be welcome to stay in the cottage indefinitely.

His mother started to refuse, but he held up a hand. "Mom, it's okay to say 'yes.' When I get back we'll move your stuff in. You'll need to get some food, but you're welcome to stay as long as you want. Do you have a bag with you?"

His mother reached out and took the key with one hand and patted his cheek with the other. "I do. I didn't screw up so badly, did I? At least my boys are good men."

"Not sure about that, Mom. I was a dick to Kendall. I thought I was protecting myself, but she was right. I'm a coward. This time she was the brave one and I let her down. Maybe I always have. I mean, I was the one left behind, right? The wounded and abandoned husband. The only time I went after her I ended up leaving when I saw her up on that stage."

"You didn't know any better. I don't think I was any kind of example as a mother."

"No. It wasn't your fault. It was mine. I was afraid of what might happen if she came home with me. What if she realized that I wasn't enough? What if she gave up her career and she ended up resenting me? And now she's lost so much. Our time might have passed." And the knife that had been sitting in his ribs since Kendall walked out the door again twisted in deeper.

"Oh honey, when I talked to her she sounded so sad, so

lonely. She acted brave like she always does." They both chuckled. That was Kendall, all right, putting up a fearless front no matter what. "But there was something hollow about our conversation."

"I might be too late. I don't know what I'm flying into. I don't know what she wants or even if there's any chance left for two broken people like us. But I'm going after her. Because that's what she deserves."

He had to try. He had to try and set them both free from this endless guilt and fear, even if that meant he didn't get the girl.

DAMIAN DIDN'T MAKE his flight out to Los Angeles, nor did he make any other flight that night. A soup-like fog had rolled in making it impossible for prop planes to fly out of their small regional airport. After hours of debate with himself on whether or not he should call Kendall, he opted not to. It was too late and it would only complicate things further if he said he'd be there and then he didn't make it. Or, even worse, if she told him not to come.

When morning finally rolled around and the fog dissipated, Damian had already been awake for hours. He boarded the plane looking just like a man who'd spent the night on the floor of the airport because the benches at the gate were too narrow for his big-ass body. And while only slightly less enthusiastic about getting to Kendall, he was concerned about how his sudden appearance at her meeting in his current state might look to both her and the label execs, so he'd called her and left a message.

He'd kept it to a simple *Hey, sweetheart, I'm on my way. I'll call you when I get in.*

But by the time he'd landed and checked his phone for messages, the meeting had already started and he was at least forty-five minutes away, if he got lucky and didn't hit traffic. He had two missed calls from Kendall but no voicemail. She did send a text with the address of the record label offices and another that said, *See you soon xoxox.*

Damian's heart beat harder in his chest, so hard it felt like it might jump from his body. She wanted him there. Or, at the very least, she was resigned to his arrival. That was good.

Very good.

What wasn't good was that he had no idea what her options were and if she'd be receptive to his plan, because he didn't really know what she wanted. He'd replayed every conversation they'd had over the last couple weeks for any sign or hint at what Kendall wanted and he was still at a loss. She said she loved him. She even said she'd missed home and that life on the road had been harder than she'd expected. But did that add up to her wanting to move back home with him?

Damian wanted her to be happy. Not in some kind of

trite martyring way where he could live out his days as the tragic hermit farmer of Blackberry Cove while she traveled all over the world as a famous entertainer. But the kind of happy that would give her roots and bring her joy. He would love her enough for the both of them. He would love her enough to let her go. For real this time.

When he pulled up to the building and took the elevator up to the correct floor his stomach was in knots. Doing the right thing was getting more and more complicated the later it got. The last thing he wanted to do was swoop into her meeting and make it worse and not better. But his need to stand by her and support her no matter what outweighed anything else.

So he took a deep breath and let the office assistant announce him into the meeting. Five sets of eyes stared at him as he stepped into the room. The knots in his stomach tightened and his heart beat faster because only one face, the one that mattered, smiled his way.

Kendall. His gorgeous, amazingly talented wife. And that was what he needed. He remembered why he was there and what he was supposed to do. He wasn't out of his element, because she *was* his element.

After brief introductions around the table, Damian asked to speak with Kendall privately before they continued with the meeting.

"Mr. Sloane, we're glad you could finally make it," Kendall's rep said. "However, we're running short on time and are ready to conclude negotiations…which, of course, you're welcome to observe."

"Morgan, is it?" The rep nodded curtly. "I'll respect your need to expedite these proceedings. But Kendall is without representation as she has neither an attorney or agent present, so I think it would be in your best interest if she takes a couple minutes to confer with me privately." Kendall stared at him, her eyes narrowed and her jaw tight. Tough shit. She could do this all on her own. He knew that. But she didn't have to. And that was the fucking point.

"Look, Mr. Sloane," said the branch VP. "It's great that you're here, but Kendall is a professional. She doesn't need her hubby to come to her rescue in a business meeting. So—"

"No she doesn't. We are business partners though and what happens here affects our business as well so if you could give us a couple minutes, five tops, that would be appreciated." Grumbling, all four executives left the room and gathered just outside the door before Damian shut it.

"What the hell was that show of testosterone, Damian?" Kendall stood and faced him. "I don't need you to rescue me—"

"No you don't. But I didn't want you to have to do this alone," he said reaching out to cradle her face.

"They can see you through the window…"

"Fuck them. I'm your husband, I'm allowed to touch you." He stroked her cheek and moved his hand around to the back of her neck. "And I'm allowed to do this," he said pulling her close and kissing her.

Without pulling away completely, Kendall looked up at him, her eyes watery and her cheeks flushed. "Why *are* you here, Damian?" she asked and bit her bottom lip. They both sat facing each other and he took her hands, surprised at the shake in them. Kendall was more nervous than she let on.

"To sit by your side and support you, no matter what." It really was that simple. "What are your options?"

She squeezed his hands with her own and breathed deeply, the air lifting her long wispy bangs from her face. "They want me to record another album and tour."

"What do you want to do?" Finally. This is where they were. At the question that would determine the course of their lives. "What will make you happy, Kendall? Really happy?"

"I want to be involved in music if I can, like writing or something. But I really just want to...I...I want..."

"What, baby, what do you want?" The knots in his stomach began to loosen, unfurling and changing into something else altogether. "I promise you that I won't do anything to hold you back. I will support you and wait for you."

He watched the shadows move over her face. She was still afraid of opening herself up and trusting him, afraid of rejection, so he leaned forward and took her face in his hands.

"I love you, Kendall Kelly. With every fucking cell in my

body. I have belonged to you since I was seventeen. I'm not going anywhere. I'm not going back to being bitter. You changed all that. You made me realize that what we had was special and unique. You are the one for me. The only one. Forever. And I want it to work, but I won't sacrifice your happiness anymore. And if you need to tour, then go knowing that I support you in every way. And when you need me to come for you I will. But I need to tell you one other thing. I want to buy into Kelly Family Farms."

Kendall frowned. "I don't understand."

"The farm is yours. It's your heritage and it came from your family. I would like to give you the money to buy out your contract, if that's what you want, or to do whatever you want with it. But I want it to be my buy-in." He pulled out the envelope in his pocket and handed it to her. "I'm going to wait in the lobby for you. You finish your meeting and come to me." He stood, kissed her cheek. "I love you."

Damian walked out the door. "She's all yours. Good luck," he said as he passed the anxious group waiting outside the conference room.

Chapter Fourteen

WHEN KENDALL EMERGED from that conference room almost two hours later she expected to find a message on her phone from Damian that he'd meet her at the hotel. Instead she found him in the lobby as promised. Sitting on a sofa with his tablet and a notebook spread out in front of him he looked every bit the successful cowboy businessman he was in his rumpled suit with the tie long removed and the jacket hanging over the arm of the sofa.

Such a ruggedly handsome man with those glowing hazel eyes framed in thick lashes, and the dark hair falling over his forehead. She had loved this man nearly her entire life and now he was hers. Finally.

At least that's what it had sounded like back in that conference room when he'd held her hands in his and stared into her eyes, practically begging her to believe him, trust him. He looked up from his work and a slow smile curved his lips when he spotted her. She froze mid-step for a moment before his chuckle snapped her out of her stupor. Quickly he gathered his belongings and threw them in his backpack before standing and pulling her toward the elevator.

They held hands, but said nothing. She felt as nervous as a high schooler on her first big date...not unlike the one she'd gone on with Damian years before. The conversation they were about to have was a biggie, no way around it. Everything they'd been through, everything they'd endured was merely practice for what lay in front of them.

The Uber that Damian had called from the lobby was sitting at the curb and delivered them back to her hotel within twenty very long minutes. When they finally made it to her room he released her hand and pushed her toward the bed.

"Damian, stop. We need to talk." He pushed on her shoulder and she sat on the bed where he kneeled in front of her and took her boots off.

"So talk, baby," he said and sat next to her on the bed. How could he be so damn calm when there was a tornado of emotions ripping her insides apart?

"Don't you want to know what happened?"

"Of course I do. But I want you to tell me when you're ready," he said, confidence oozing from him.

"How can you be so calm? Ugh. I gave them the check, Damian." She clutched her fists at her sides.

He laughed, an arrogant chuckle. Like he knew she was going to give them the money, like there hadn't been any question that she wanted to go back with him. "You knew that?"

"I had hoped you would. I think you made it clear you

wanted to come home."

"I did."

"You did."

She cleared her throat, which suddenly felt dry. "I, uh, told them I'd be interested in writing songs, but not recording them." She shifted her hands to her lap and looked down.

"That's great, baby."

"Really? That's all you have to say?"

"Nope," he said and dropped to his knees with a small box in his hand.

"Damian. I already have a wedding ring."

"I know." He flipped the box open to reveal a platinum charm bracelet with one single charm, a jeweled goat, dangling from it. "This is more of a promise, Kendall. I'm going to buy you a charm to mark every important event in our lives moving forward." He pulled it from the blue-velvet-lined box and fastened it around her wrist. The simple action felt like so much more. It was a promise and a commitment and an anchor to her home and her man and the life she was meant to have. No more running.

"It's beautiful. But there might be one more charm we need to add," she said quietly.

"And which one is that?" he asked, raising a brow.

"I've been sick to my stomach the past couple days. On a whim I bought a test and took it before I left this morning." He grabbed her hand and held it tightly still on his knees in front of her.

"And…" He reached up to touch her face, like he always did, seeking that deeper connection.

"I don't know. I was afraid to look. It's in there." She held her breath and gestured to the bathroom. Damian jumped up and pulled her to the bathroom until she dug in her heels and stopped. "What if it's positive, Damian?"

He turned around and wrapped his arms around her, pulling her into that safe place of love and comfort and Damian. "Then we'll be parents, Kendall." He stroked his hands down her hair and she leaned in to him.

"But what about what my grandma said?"

"Probably bullshit. Even if it's not, it doesn't matter." His mom had told her that her grandma's claims were wrong, but hearing Damian say so was more important. And the relief that flooded through her body was like sunshine and waterfalls and butterflies all wrapped up in one big giant pink bow. "Ready?"

Kendall smiled against his chest, before turning and walking into the bathroom. The simple plastic wand sat on the edge of the sink, taunting her. Did she deserve to get everything? Was she going to get her happily ever after in the form of this incredible man and a baby? Her own family?

Damian squeezed her hand again and kissed the back of her neck. "If not now, then later. And if not later, then we have each other. Forever, Kendall."

He was right, of course. He always was. "I can't look and

it's probably too early and I don't feel sick now and I'm still pretty young and we just got back together." Everything froze and narrowed down to Damian's big hand as it reached down and picked up that little stick. She studied his face as he stared at, but he gave nothing away.

Finally a grin so big it stretched his face into one she hadn't seen since he was a teen, and he asked, "What does a plus sign mean?"

Then he dragged her to the bed and spent the next two days showing her exactly how he felt about her.

Epilogue

KENDALL KELLY WAS home.

She finished changing her infant daughter, smoothed her strawberry blonde curls with her hand and picked her up from the changing table. Cradling Sophia in her arms, Kendall walked toward the noise coming from her recently finished living room. The room was filled with people, people she loved laughing and drinking and talking.

Delilah sat on one of the couches speaking to Damian's brother, Duncan, who had come home for the weekend. Damian's mom laughed at something one of the girl's from the shop was saying. A group of the farm's workers, including Coleman and Samantha, were circling a table full of appetizers and desserts. Kendall continued out to the big house's grand porch and found her husband sitting on a chair laughing with Colin and two friends that Damian had recently reconnected with.

In her husband's arms was the other man she'd been looking for, her son, Evan. She marveled as her husband's large hand stroked their son's matching dark hair. That she could have missed all this—the family, the love, the one—

was a startling realization. She could have missed her own life if she had continued to run from her own fear instead of take it on. Instead she won the lottery. In the year since Damian had brought her back home they'd settled into a busy, but infinitely rewarding life. Her husband had worked like a madman on both the farm and renovating her grandmother's old house. He insisted on creating the home their children would grow up in and he and Kendall would grow old in.

Today had been their housewarming slash vow renewal and they'd invited just about everyone they knew to the simple, but meaningful ceremony. Of course, a couple fussy babies helped a lot in keeping the exchange short and sweet. Life was exhausting with two busy babies, renovations, and the farm to run, but having her mother-in-law in their cottage was endlessly helpful. Not only was Evelyn an incredible grandmother and always helpful, but she had become like a mother to Kendall. She filled a dark void in Kendall with love and acceptance and kindness that she had never known from another woman other than Delilah.

When Damian looked up from his conversation and caught her staring at him, he laughed and called to her. She paused for a moment before moving to sit on the wide arm of his chair.

"Hey, baby," he said and patted her leg, before stealing the baby in her arms.

"Baby hog." She laughed. Because that's what she did these days—she laughed. A lot. Sure there were still tears and there were times she felt overwhelmed, but every time her husband was there to catch her before she fell.

And as she sat there on her glossy new porch with her husband, her children, and their friends and families, Kendall watched the sun lower in the sky and touch the hill at the edge of their little valley. The way the sky was painted in vibrant colors before it began to tuck itself in for the evening was the very last thing she remembered that night before falling asleep in Damian's arms, exhausted from lovemaking. And the last thing she felt was the press of his lips on her shoulder before he said, "I will love you forever, Kendall."

The End

The Blackberry Cove
Cowboys Series

Book 1: *Punk Rock Cowgirl*

Book 2: *Big, Bad Cowboy Soldier*

Book 3: *The Rebel Cowboy's Bride*

Available now at your favorite online retailer!

More Books
by Kasey Lane

Beautiful Wreck

Available now at your favorite online retailer!

About the Author

Award-winning author Kasey Lane writes sexy romances featuring alpha males and the strong women that bring them to their knees. A California transplant, she lives with her high school crush turned husband, two smart, but devilish kids, two dumb-as-rocks Papillons, and a bunch of bossy chickens in the lush Oregon forest. Visit her on line at www.kaseylane.com where you'll find her swearing too much and talking about hockey, music, and happily ever afters.

Thank you for reading

Punk Rock Cowgirl

If you enjoyed this book, you can find more from all our great authors at TulePublishing.com, or from your favorite online retailer.

TULE
PUBLISHING